TEXAS

BOUND

by

Arnold McKay

This book is a work of fiction. Names, characters, places, and incidents are either the product of the author's imagination or are used fictitiously. Any resemblance to actual persons, living or dead, events or locales is entirely coincidental.

Note for Librarians: A cataloguing record for this book is available from Library and Archives Canada at www.collectionscanada.ca/amicus.indes-e.html

ISBN 978-0-9879535-1-3

Thank you to Deb and Lorne Lausen for
the front cover photo.

Books by Arnold McKay

Wyoming
Texas Bound
Dying Bequest

About the Author

Arnold McKay is the author of Wyoming,
Dying Bequest and Texas Bound.
He lives in British Columbia, Canada
with his wife and is currently at work on his
fourth novel.

Chapter 1

Today it all came to a head. First, John came thundering into the yard on a lathered horse. That in itself was not unusual. He was always hard on his horses.

He quickly stripped the gear from his horse, saddled another and then rode off towards town without coming inside.

When he rode past the house, it looked as if he had a black eye. Ben had the feeling that John had finally laid a hand on his brother.

John was forever picking on Jed. Up until now, it had all been verbal abuse. Jed would let it slide and it seemed that John had the feeling that Jed was afraid of him.

Jed, his second son was hard to understand but Ben had studied him since he was a boy and he knew there was a lot more to Jed than met the eye.

It was too bad he couldn't leave the ranch in Jed's care but there was that old promise he had made to his grandfather that he would leave the ranch to his oldest son, the only great grandchild his grandfather had lived to see.

He made the mistake of telling John when he was twelve years old what his grandfather had said. Now it seemed that John was trying to boss the ranch crew and Jed, too but Jed didn't need bossing. He knew what needed to be done and he just went ahead and did it.

The cowhands were always happy to follow Jed without him so much as giving a direct order. They could feel the qualities in Jed the same as Ben could.

Jed was always a quiet, slow moving boy. Some, including John, thought him slow and awkward. Ben had studied on this and he realized Jed could do more work at his own pace than any man on the ranch.

Jed was tall and gangly like Holly's father. Maybe not quite so tall but the same long arms that were hard to get sleeves long enough to cover. Since Holly passed away, Jed had started buying his shirts in size large to make the sleeves long enough. The shirts fit too loose and made him look like a scarecrow but Ben had seen him washing up after work with his shirt off. He'd seen the wide shoulders and long muscles of his back and arms. He had also known that someday John would feel the strength of those arms and now he was quite sure that day had come.

Later, he would call aside one of the old ranch hands and find out what he could about what had happened. Maybe it wasn't that serious but he had a feeling the time had come for him to make some decisions.

After supper, Ben sat on the porch waiting for the men to come out of the cook house. He called for Gimpy to come and sit a spell with him. Ben saw him hesitate, not wanting to get into the middle of a family matter but Gimpy knew Ben was still the boss after all, though he didn't do chores much anymore. Gimpy limped his way to the porch and sat down.

Ben gave him time to get his pipe lit then he asked him straight out what had happened out on the range that day.

"Well, Ben, what happened was John got the surprise of his life. You know how he's always bossin' Jed around? Jed usually takes whatever orders John dishes out and then mostly he does them his own way.

"Today John was lamentin' because Del and Rose were

planting crops around their place. Seems Del plowed up a few acres for corn and wheat this year ... put a pole fence around it. John said he had a good mind to teach Del a lesson ... like run some cattle through his fence. Jed told him he would do no such thing and if he ever tried, he'd stop him.

"Well, John never heard him talk back before and he laid a hand on Jed and yanked him up. The next thing John knew, he was flat on his back and then he went for his gun. If we hadn't held him, I swear he would have shot Jed even though Jed wasn't armed.

"If I was you, Ben, I'd separate those two. I know you promised your grandfather to give the ranch to John when you're gone. If I was you, I'd take back some of the authority you seem to have given John. I don't know what you can do to keep them apart but you'd better come up with something or you'll either find yourself with only one son or none at all. I suspect Jed can handle a gun at least as well as John although he hardly ever carries one. One way or another, you'll lose both boys if it comes to a shootin'."

"Well, Gimpy, you've given it to me straight. I kind of suspected as much. I've watched Jed since he was a boy when everyone thought he was slow and awkward. Over the years, I've noticed that if he needs speed, he can generate speed. I've also noticed that he can do everything with his left hand that he can do with his right. Did you ever notice that he uses a hammer with either hand? I've even seen him shoot left handed just as naturally as right.

"He's a gentle boy most times. He was so considerate of his mother when she was sick. Brought fresh flowers in from work most days so she would have somethin' pretty in her room; sat with her many nights toward the end. He and Rose had the hard part. I couldn't stay with her very long. It was too hard.

"It's been a long, hard three years since Holly died and I guess I've let things slide around here. Depended on the boys to do what's needed. Seems I have to make some changes. I don't expect John will be back for work tomorrow so you and the boys take your orders from Jed till I get this thing figured out."

Later, after Gimpy went to the bunkhouse, Ben sat alone on the porch till close to midnight.

First he thought back over the years and how the situation had gotten to this point. He had gone north after receiving a letter from his long lost mother to rescue her from a bad situation.

After a stint there as Deputy Sheriff, he had married Holly Benson. They returned to the *Rocking O* the following spring to find his grandfather, Jed sidelined with a bout of pneumonia. It had helped to bring him around when he found that he now had two women to wait on him ... Holly and Ben's mother, Jane. His grandfather had lived another two years, long enough to see his first great grandson and make that regrettable request that Ben leave the *Rocking O* in the hands of John.

Before his grandfather died, Jane requested that he sell her back the section of land that she and Ben's father had lived on before his father's accident saying she just needed something tangible to leave behind for Ben after she was gone.

Eight years later, Ben's mother passed away, leaving him not only the section of land but most of the money she had gotten from her land up north. That money was still in a bank account in Cheyenne.

Finally, deciding that he would have to sacrifice the rest of his remaining years to prevent the blow up that would soon come between his sons, he went to bed.

In the morning, Ben sent word to Jed to come to the office before he rode out. After the men mounted up and rode out of the ranch yard, he saw Jed making his way towards the house.

Thinking this might be easier outside, he stepped out to the porch and sat down.

"Papa, I reckon you want to see me about what happened yesterday."

"Yes, Son, and I want you to know I don't blame you in any way. I was up half the night going over what I might do to help the situation. I've decided the only sure way to keep you and John from having trouble is to keep you apart.

"First, I want you to go to Texas for me. We need some new bulls. Something not local. We've been tradin' breeding stock with neighbours for too long with nobody keeping track of blood lines. We should get a dozen at least ... young Herefords.

"Tomorrow, before you head out, I'll give you a bank draft for what money you'll need. I'll write to the bank in Cheyenne. You'll have to ride through there and pick it up. I don't know where you'll find the stock but I'll leave that challenge up to you. Maybe start asking as soon as you get to Cheyenne.

"Now the next thing I want is for you to tell me what you think of Rose's husband. You knew I didn't cotton to the marriage and nobody talks to me much about it. They been gettin' along alright?"

"Well, Papa, I drop by when I'm up there. Del's fixed the place up what he can afford and Rose seems happy enough, considering she lost her Ma and sorta lost her Pa when she got married. You probably know you got a granddaughter and another baby on the way. Del figures he can make that place into a money maker someday but I don't think John is going to let that happen."

"Well, maybe John won't have anything to say about it. That place is not part of the *Rocking O*, although it does belongs to me. It was my father and mother who started out there. Mother owned it when she died and she left it to me. I think perhaps I misjudged Del Ramsey. Do you think I'd be

11

welcome if I was to take a ride up there?"

"Papa, you'd be as welcome as the flowers of springtime. I guess I know from the way you're talking, Papa, what you have in mind. Don't let John know your plans till I get back."

"Okay, Son. Don't work too hard today. Get ready for that trip and if John gets back before you go, just stay away from him."

As Jed walked back to the bunkhouse, he decided the best thing he could do was ride the range the rest of the day. If John came back, he'd most likely be hungover and quarrelsome. He quickly made up his bedroll, assembled what camping gear he would need on the trip tomorrow and then rode south. He'd check the water holes and fences in that area and do some thinking about what lay ahead for him.

Up till now, he'd lived his life for his mother and father. He knew in his own heart that if he hadn't stayed around to see that the work was done after his mother died, the ranch would have suffered great losses from winter kill and rustlers. John spent two or three days a week in town which was maybe a good thing. The men didn't like taking orders from him.

How John would make out while he was away, he had no idea but it might be wise for his father to step in for a week or two even though John would resent it. John had lost face with the ranch hands yesterday, especially when he started to draw that gun. If Fred hadn't kicked his hand when he did, things could have been a lot different.

That was something he would have to tell his father about. John wouldn't take lightly that Fred had stopped him.

Jed was glad he hadn't been armed yesterday. His reflexes might have caused him to draw and fire before he could stop himself. Some time ago, he had come to realize that he was very fast when circumstances demanded. He didn't think, he just acted.

Well, tomorrow he'd be out in the big, wide world by himself. He'd find out how he stacked up. Tonight, he would get in late and since he slept in the bunkhouse with the men and John slept in the house, they probably wouldn't meet. First thing in the morning, he'd talk to his father alone and then ride out.

When John came riding in later that evening, Ben decided there were some things that could not be put off. As soon as John came in, he called him into the office.

"Well, Pop, I suppose you want to talk about that little dust up Jed and I had yesterday?"

"Well, I guess it could have been a lot more than a little dust up if the boys hadn't held you back. What were you thinkin', drawing a gun on your brother?"

"He's always makin' me look bad in front of the men. Yesterday, he challenged me outright. When I started to set him straight about who ran things, he knocked me down in front of the men."

"There's one thing I want to make plain, John. Until I'm dead, I'll make whatever decisions I see fit. First, don't go near Rose and Del's place until I say so. I'm riding up there tomorrow. I want to find out how they're making out."

"That Del is startin' to fence like he owns the place. First thing you know, he'll have us fenced off from water!"

"And, John, I've decided some breathing room is needed between you and Jed so I'm sending Jed to buy some new bulls. We've used this local stock so long, they must be gettin' inbred. Meant to go myself but I've got more urgent business to attend to here."

As John left the office, he wondered what Ben had in mind. He hadn't taken much interest in anything since Holly died.

Then Rose up and married that Del Ramsay though she didn't have much choice. She was so big with child, everyone knew.

Anyway he'd be clear of Jed for awhile. He was always finding some reason to countermand his orders and make it look like he ran things.

The next morning, Jed waited till John rode out with the men, remaining in the bunkhouse preparing what he had to take with him. When he got everything together, he realized he'd have to take along a pack horse. With what he was taking from here and what he would have to pick up in Cheyenne, it was way too much to carry behind his saddle.

When he went up to the house, Ben was already in the office.

"Well, Papa, I think I'm all ready. I guess I should get on the road. It's a full day to Cheyenne so it will be tomorrow morning before I get to the bank. I think I'll ride all the way to Texas. The railroad is kind of round about and I might get what I'm after closer to home."

"Well, I'm goin' to leave it to you, Jed. Don't rush. I've headed things off here for a time and when you get back, there might be some changes around here. One thing's sure, I can't have you and John at each others throats any longer. I've decided to visit Rose and Del today and tomorrow I'm going to Cheyenne myself. So you tell Albright at the bank he can expect me the day after tomorrow. Take care, Son and come back safe."

Jed set out with mixed feelings. It was the first time he was sent out to do anything as important as this and he wondered if he would be up to the task.

From the talk he had heard from old cowhands, it must be four or five hundred miles just to get to the Texas border. He might have to swap horses to keep going steady.

Then again he might find what he wanted before he got there. Most likely it was ranch country all the way south. One thing for sure, he would have to freight whatever livestock he bought back home. It would be expensive but necessary. The railroad lines were built east to west so he would have to ship east until the tracks joined up with the line going west to Cheyenne.

Every step of the way south, he would have to ask directions and check for breeding bulls that might be for sale. Had his father foreseen how much trouble it might be to find a dozen bulls in a small enough area to be feasible? Nobody he knew in their area had ever thought of such a scheme. It probably would have been easier to head east by train, get what bulls he could wherever he could and ship them back to Cheyenne by train. It must be that his father had something more in mind for this trip.

He arrived in Cheyenne in the late afternoon, booked his room at the hotel and had supper in the dining room. He'd see Mr. Albright at the bank in the morning and then get started south.

Chapter 2

Ben wasn't looking forward to this meeting. He had planned to see Rose with some misgivings. Though he had kept Del on the payroll and he'd let the couple settle into the old homestead place, he had made no secret that he didn't approve of their marriage.

As far as he knew, Del had looked after the *Rocking O* cattle on the old homestead. At least he hadn't heard any complaints and John would surely have taken the opportunity if there had been reason.

As he rode into the yard, Rose came to the door with a small face peeking out from behind her dress tail. So this would be his first grandchild and by the looks of Rose, it wouldn't be long before he'd have another.

"Hello, Papa. What brings you up here? Checking up on Del's fencing?"

"No, nothing of the sort. I guess you must have heard about the quarrel between Jed and John over the fence."

"Yes, we heard though I won't say who told us. Won't you get down and come in. Del's out riding but he'll be in at noon. He won't leave me alone too long right now."

Ben stepped down and as he started toward the house, the little face disappeared and he heard scurrying feet going for a corner somewhere, afraid of her grandfather. What a sorry mess he'd made. Anyway, there was still time to set thing's right but he wanted to talk to Del first and see what his plans were.

As he stepped through the door, he realized what a difference Rose had made of the old place. The main difference he supposed, it was clean. Before Rose and Del moved here, the place was used as a stopover for the men when they worked in the area. No one felt responsible for keeping it clean so it had become a pig sty. Now it looked comfortable, although small. It started his memory back to when he was a boy.

"Sit down, Papa. I'll get some coffee and maybe you'd like a doughnut. Lunch won't be for an hour or more yet. What brought you up here this morning? I'd heard you didn't ride much anymore."

"Well, Rose, this trouble between Jed and John has me worried sick and Jed suggested I should make a move to mend some fences. I sent Jed on an errand to keep him away for a month or two. While he's gone I need to figure out where we all stand. I used to have a family but since Holly died, the family has died with her. I know this thing between Jed and John hasn't just started but it's gotten much worse recently. It could have been held off I suppose, if I hadn't sat by and let them take the reins.

You know that I promised grandfather I'd leave the ranch to John one day. Well, I'm sorry I made that promise. Jed's the one that's made the ranch what it is and I don't know if John can keep the place up without him but I have to send Jed away or they'll destroy each other."

"Well, Papa, I've known that for a long time. John didn't let you see all the things between himself and Jed but I've seen it since I was a kid. Ever since he found out he was to inherit the *Rocking O*, he's Lorded it over Jed. I sure hate for Jed to go away. He's the only steady friend Del and I have had since we married."

"Well, that's enough talk about my troubles for now. Have you been happy, Rose?"

"I could be a lot happier if we had more company or if we could drop by the ranch now and again. Del's been good to me if that's what you want to know. He gets frustrated sometimes, riding alone day after day, looking after someone else's cattle. He'd like to put in more crops. He's trying some oats this year figuring since no one else plants any, he can sell them as horse feed. He hasn't got what he needs to process them he says but at least if he gets a few bushels he'll know whether it's worth while. He had corn last year, sold it to the livery in town but it really wasn't enough to count much."

"Well, it surely seems he's tryin' and that's what I came to find out, among other things. I've told John to stay away from here and cause no problems for Del and for the next while, I'm going to be the boss again at least till Jed gets back."

Just then Ben heard Del ride in and he must have been anxious about what was taking place in the house because he left his horse by the corral gate and came straight to the house. He arrived at the door with a scowl on his face.

Rose took one look at him and took the situation in hand.

"It ain't what you think, Del so calm down. Papa's just making a visit to tell us John won't be bothering us. This year at least."

"Rose asked me to stay and eat so maybe we should turn our horses loose and give them some feed."

When they had that chore done, Ben leaned up to the corral fence and loaded his pipe. Del, sensing that Ben had something on his mind, did likewise.

"Del, I can see you've done some work around here and you've done alright by my cattle. I guess you've been puttin' in some long days. What would be your plans if you owned this section?"

"Well, I've done enough plantin' to know that corn and

grain will grow here. Some areas could be irrigated, too. People around here don't raise anything that can't walk to water on it's own so I'd guess there would be a market for most anything a man could get a crop of. Sold a few bushels to the livery stable last fall but I've got no machine for shellin' corn or thrashin' wheat. Did it by hand. This year, I got too much. Maybe I'll try to sell the corn, cob and all."

"Del, I got to tell you, I didn't like it when you up and married Rose. Maybe I was just needin' some female company around me after Holly died. Anyhow, this dust up between John and Jed has brought me to my senses. It seems that if things are left to go on, I won't have a family at all. I've sent Jed to Texas for a new breed of bulls. I could have found some closer but I need time to sort through some things and I can't do that and worry that those boys might shoot each other. I've given John orders to leave you alone up here and when Jed gets back, I'll get the family together and make something more permanent.

"Don't worry about your work going to waste here, Del. I like your ideas and I think you could make this section pay. Well, we'd best go inside. Rose is probably thinkin' the worst being as how we haven't spoken two words to each other these last two years."

As they came to the door, his granddaughter turned to run for her hiding place but Rose caught her and turned her back to the table.

"Don't try to talk to her, Papa. She's really shy. The only one she ever sees is Jed. Give her time. Her curiosity will get the better of her eventually."

After they had eaten, Ben asked Del to stay. He had something to say to both of them.

"Now you two are wondering about my change of attitude but I assure you what I'm going to say is true. First off, this section of land here doesn't belong to the *Rocking O* Ranch but it does belong to me. I inherited it from Mother, not my grandfather. John doesn't know that and I hope he doesn't find out for the next month or so. I like Del's ideas about farmin' here and I think it could be made to pay. Meantime, Del needs to continue getting his paycheck for looking after our stock so keep what I'm saying quiet for now."

By the time Ben was ready to leave, his granddaughter had started to study him with her big, brown eyes. Ben would have liked to pick her up but he realized it would take more time. Rose did manage to get her to wave goodby as he rode away. Tomorrow, he'd go to Cheyenne and stay as long as it took to get the business done.

The next morning in Cheyenne, Jed ate breakfast at the hotel and then asked directions to the bank. As he was crossing the street, he had to hurry out of the way of a stage leaving town in what he assumed was south bound. He hadn't realized that stages would be running but he supposed that with the railroad going mostly east to west, the stages still carried passengers north and south. Maybe he'd be better off going by stage. He'd check into it after he left the bank. It was a wonder his father hadn't mentioned it but then again his father hadn't travelled much, either.

He got in immediately to see Mr. Albright and was given a bank draft for twelve hundred dollars plus five hundred dollars in cash.

"Ben says in this note he'll be in himself tomorrow. Do you know what he might be wanting?"

"No, I don't. It's some last minute idea he had and since I was all packed, he didn't want to hold me up. I don't know if Pa says in that note what this money's for but I'm heading out to find some new bulls, Herefords that he wants. You any idea who might be raisin' breeding stock?"

"No, Jed, I don't. Most ranchers around here are just starting to use Herefords. I'm sure no one is set up to supply anyone else."

"Well, I'm headin' for Texas. I might find some before I get there."

"I'll tell you what. I'm going to write you a reference letter. Now, anyplace you stop that has a bank, you show them that letter. Bankers make it their business to know who's doing what in their area and maybe someone can help you out. Drop by this afternoon and I'll have it ready."

"That's mighty kind. I've decided to stay in town today. I think I'll check out stage travel. I came prepared to ride and camp out but I see they have stages goin' south. I could stop a day any place that looked promising and pick up the stage again the next day."

"Well, I think you have the right idea. With the stages changing horses every fifteen or twenty miles, you'll make better time and get hot meals at the way station, too."

After he left the bank, he went to the stage station to check schedules and get what information he could. The agent gave him what information he had for as far south as he was familiar with and told him a stage headed south every day, same time as this morning. The first real stopover would be Fort Collins, about forty miles south. The next leg of the journey was a fourteen hour run to Denver. He advised Jed to check at the Denver station for information before going on.

On his way to the livery stable, he stopped at a store and bought a duffel bag. He'd have to lighten his load a great deal. Now he wouldn't need his food and camping gear. He'd have to find a place to cache what he couldn't take.

The livery owner agreed to keep the horses and feed them in exchange for their usage while Jed was gone. He also gave permission to leave his gear behind so Jed gave him what food he had in his pack.

He stowed his spare clothes and personal belongings in the duffel bag and then wrote a note to his father explaining his change of plans. He then went back to the hotel and arranged for a bath. Tomorrow would be a long day.

TEXAS BOUND   Arnold McKay

The following day was a long, tedious ride. Get in the stage, go fast for fifteen miles, change horses and go again at top speed to the next stage depot and stop to have a noon meal about one o'clock. Then get in the stage once more, go like heck for another fifteen miles, change horses and go again.

They arrived at Fort Collin's at six o'clock and Jed was glad to get out of the coach. That idea he had of laying over a day in each town was starting to look good.

The next day, he checked around at the bank, the Sheriff's office and the stage station. No one knew where he might find Hereford bulls. Not many ranchers had them and they certainly didn't have a dozen to part with.

The next day, he boarded the stage for Denver with another long tedious day.

It was the same story in Denver. No one knew of Hereford bulls for sale. He even received some strange looks for asking such a question.

At the next stop, he didn't lay over. The driver from his first day had caught up with them by this time and invited Jed to ride up top. At least he'd see some scenery and feel the breeze.

Four days later, he arrived at Raton, New Mexico. By this time, he was starting to wonder if his father had any idea about the distance to Texas or any place in Texas. But then from what he'd been told, he was heading for the largest state in the union. How was he ever going to find twelve breeding bulls there? He decided he'd make no more stopovers till he got to Texas.

Finally, in Amarillo, he got his first break. While he was asking the bartender in the Last Chance about Hereford bulls, he was overheard by a scruffy looking cowboy making his way through the free lunch.

After the bartender replied that he didn't know where he

could find bulls in Amarillo, this cowboy moved over beside him and said he could tell him where he could buy what he wanted. Jed figured he was being hit on for a drink in exchange for some phoney information but he'd come up empty every place else so he might as well spend a quarter on a drink and see what happened.

He asked the bartender for a bottle and two glasses. The man gave him the items and also a wink as much as to say, good luck!

As they sat at the table and poured their drinks, the fellow introduced himself as Ricky Dansen. Jed told him his name and asked him how come he knew where there was Hereford bulls for sale.

"Well, Mr. Owens, I worked with an outfit down below Richardson. Had a nice place, Joe did. Well, one day he just keeled over there in the yard. Heart attack and only fifty five.

"The only kin was a daughter about twenty-five. Things might of been alright if she'd a been left alone. She had three good enough ranch hands plus old Rolly. No tough men you understand, just cowboys like myself. But then there was a horse rancher in the area started showin' up. Now Miss Ellen, she sure didn't cotton to him but he sure was persistent. Finally, me and Chad Watson got beat up and told to leave town. Not by this Artie Smith but we knew who was behind it. We might of stayed by Miss Ellen, but she told us she couldn't pay our wages much longer and maybe it would be best if we leave. So far as I know, she's still there with just old Rolly. He's so old and stove up, not likely they'll bother him any. I reckon this Artie Smith is just waitin' her out. When I left, all the calf crop was unbranded and not neutered. So if things haven't changed, there should be maybe sixty young bulls just waiting to be culled out."

"That sure sounds like a good story, Ricky. Have another drink. It's worth that much just to hear you talk."

"I'm not talkin' just because I want to bend your ear a

23

little. I sure would like for someone to step in there who could take that Artie Smith down a peg. I don't like one bit what he's doin' to Miss Ellen."

"Would you be interested in hiring on to guide me down there. No money mind you till we get there and I find you're telling me true. I'll supply the grub and anything we might need. What do you say to that?"

"I say, when do you want to start?"

"I guess from what you told me, the sooner the better. Let's find out when the next stage leaves."

"Where you takin' these bulls when you find some, Mr Owen? You need a hand to help?"

"Yes, I surely will. I'm taking them all the way to Cheyenne up in southern Wyoming. I guess I'll have to figure something out with the railroad."

"Well, you're in luck then. Richardson is a railroad town so we can check it out on the way through, make sure you can ship before you buy. That's where we'll leave the stage. Have to rent horses there. It's not more than one hour to the Pritchard place."

It took another three days of stage travel to reach Abilene. The next day, they boarded a train for Richardson. It eased Jed's mind about the length of time it would take to get back to Cheyenne. Although he'd be travelling east first and then back west, the train was five times faster than horses and with only occasional stops. And it would travel twenty-four hours a day.

As soon as they arrived in Richardson, Jed enquired about shipping the bulls. He was told it could be done but the miles they would have to travel might well discourage him from going ahead with the plan.

He assured the agent that he had too much invested already to stop now. He was told that when he had his purchase ready, to drop by and log on for a car going east.

The agent said they never could tell when one would be available but since it wasn't the busy time for cattle cars, he could get one in a day or two.

The next morning, they rented a couple of horses and started out early for the Pritchard ranch with Ricky insisting they wait and have breakfast in a town called Breckenridge about three miles south.

As Ricky told him, Breckenridge used to be a fair sized town but the railroad came through and put a station at Richardson and gradually everything moved to Richardson except for a few hearty souls.

As it turned out, one of those hearty souls ran a cafe and that's where Ricky turned in. The place was empty when they walked in through the door. Jed could hear some noises from what he took to be the kitchen.

As soon as they were seated, Ricky hollered.

"Sally, you've got a customer out here!"

Everything went quiet and then a face looked around the corner.

"Ricky, where did you come from? You haven't been around for months."

"Well, I was given my walkin' papers at the job and given a warning, I suppose from Artie Smith to get out of town."

"Miss Pritchard didn't fire you, did she?"

"Sort of said she couldn't pay me no more so we all left except old Rolly. Been feelin' kind of low about that. Now keep this to yourself, Sally but Mr Owens here might help Miss Ellen out a bit. He's lookin' for some Hereford bulls and Miss Ellen sure must have plenty of those. I don't reckon she's had a chance to ship anything with no help."

"Well, I don't think so. I haven't heard anything and these old hanger-oner's here are like the worst busy bodies you ever saw. There's not much I don't hear. Anyway, are you just here to see me or would you like something to eat?"

Jed spoke up then.

"Let me introduce myself. I'm Jed Owens and yes, we'd like whatever you can dish up easy for breakfast and if you can make something to carry along, we'll take that, too."

Ten minutes later, they were eating flapjacks, eggs, chopped steak and all the coffee they could hold. When Jed walked up to the counter, Sally passed him a bag of grub, enough to last at least all day. When he went to pay, she only charged for their breakfast.

"That bag full of stuff is just leftovers, some cold flapjacks from this morning and cold beef from last night. Just see what you can do for Miss Ellen. That will be pay enough."

Chapter 3

As they rode towards the Pritchard ranch, Jed wondered about this Miss Ellen as everyone seemed to call her. Ricky had mentioned her age, somewhere between twenty and twenty-five yet this Miss Ellen title almost suggested an older spinster lady. Well, he'd find out. It was only a few more miles.

They rode into the yard and were met by a black and white collie dog. He never barked, just circled the horses with his eyes taking in every move of both horses and riders. Jed noted one old timer sitting by the bunkhouse door with a double barrelled shotgun across his lap. When they stopped their horses the old man spoke.

"Well, Ricky, I see yuh ventured back. Who's that with yuh? Not trouble for Miss Ellen, I hope."

"Nope, Rolly, this is Jed Owens from way up Cheyenne way and maybe he can be some help. I'm gonna take him in and introduce him and then you can tell me what's been happening while I've been gone."

Jed and Ricky stepped onto the verandah and Ricky knocked. When the door opened, Jed, in spite of his height was looking almost eye to eye with a woman so uncommon looking, it took a moment for him to recover.

Grey eyes, that was the first thing that registered. Brown hair done up for housekeeping, the same as his mother used to do. An apron with flour smudges. Strong arms and hands to match the rest of her from which he realized was a female version of himself.

Ricky finally broke into the silence.

"Miss Ellen, this is Jed Owens. I met him in Amarillo, found out he was lookin' for Hereford bulls so I brought him along figurin' maybe he might be some help. Now, I'm goin' to talk to Rolly. If you need me for anything just holler."

"Well, Ricky, I'm delighted to see you again and if you've brought some relief here, I'm mighty grateful."

"Well, I've been ridin' with this jasper for most of a week now and I think you can trust what he says. Now, I'll let you get on with it."

"Come in, Mr Owen. I'll get you a coffee. Come on through to the kitchen and have a seat. I'm doing some bread so you must excuse me. I'll have to finish it and set it to raise."

Jed sat at the table and watched this woman who everyone, including other women called Miss Ellen. He could see now why it could happen. In spite of the large bone structure, she had a regal air about her. There was strength in her body in spite of the fact that she was far too thin. Months of worry, he supposed. Most women would have given up long ago and moved to town but here she was with her one old ranch hand too stove up to ride.

He didn't see where he could help much. Twelve head and even breeding bull prices weren't going to do much for her. Finally, she set her bread and covered it with a towel. She washed the flour off her hands, poured some coffee and sat down.

"Well, Mr Owens, what is it you can do for me as Ricky put it and what can I do for you? Ricky said something about bulls."

"That's right. I've travelled all the way from Cheyenne lookin' for Hereford bulls. I was about to give up when I met

Ricky in Amarillo. He says you have plenty."

"Well, I don't know. We only have what we always carried, maybe twenty, I guess."

"Ricky said you hadn't gotten around to the calves when he left and you'd have a bunch of yearling bulls."

"Well, lands sakes, I suppose I do. They're kind of young, though."

"I'm thinking they're just right. I'll need to ship by rail and those yearlings will travel far better than big old range bulls. Easier to load, too."

"Well, why don't you let Ricky show you around. He rode here for four years. He'll know where the stock is likely to be. When you get back, lunch will be ready. Then maybe we can talk price. No point right now till you see what you're getting."

"Well, Miss Ellen, I'll see you later. Thanks for the coffee."

As Jed stepped down from the verandah, Ricky came walking up from the bunkhouse.

"Old Rolly says they haven't had any real trouble lately except Artie Smith keeps pesterin' every few days. He's just doin' that for meanness. He knows he can't get anywhere with Miss Ellen. He's just like a vulture flyin' around after something that's dying."

"Miss Pritchard said to get you to show me around. Said you'd have an idea where the cattle would be this time of year."

"Yeh, I guess I could find what we want pretty quick. Rolly says they haven't shipped any since I left here. Miss Ellen, she can't get anyone to make the drive. It's a shame. It's only seven miles to Richardson."

"Well, let's ride out and look things over. Maybe there won't be anything left on the range."

"Rolly says he thinks they're still all there. Miss Ellen, she has the only Herefords around so if anyone was to steal any, they'd show up like a sore thumb. But I'm sure there's some makin' steak for someone's supper. Rolly says Miss Ellen, she rides out there every couple of days."

They hadn't gone very far when they started seeing cattle in the distance and Ricky turned for the nearest bunch. Jed was amazed at the size of some of the older ones. One old bull must have weighted a ton.

"That old bull there, that's old Jessop we call him. Beyond his prime now but he still noses the cows a bit. There's a couple of young bulls over there. What do you think?"

"Well, they sure look healthy enough. Kind of low to the ground for yearlings."

"Well, I tell you, Jed, they'll out weigh a Longhorn the same age by fifty pounds and that ain't all horns and hoof."

"I wonder what we'll get when we cross them with our Longhorns."

"Well, I've seen some, Jed, right here a few years ago. Ellen's father had some but he wanted purebred so he shipped them all.

"Most were red in colour, sometimes a bit of white on the back. Sometimes the build would be Longhorn, sometimes to Hereford, sometimes a pure mix. If it was me in your case, I'd try and keep the cows that were an even mix. They'd be more likely to survive the winters up north though the Hereford has a good heavy coat and if there's good feed, they fatten through the summer more than a Longhorn. Pure Hereford now, they got shorter legs. They wouldn't be able to get through the snow so well."

"Well, Ricky it's not the depth of the snow that does you real damage, it's the cold that can come at the same time. If it lasts too long it can starve cattle out."

"I don't know much about that. We don't usually get much bad weather this far south though I've heard old Rolly talk about blizzards around here."

As they rode, Jed kept watching the cattle and he could see there was plenty of bulls, one year to one and a half years old. There was really no need to go further but Ricky showed no sign of stopping so he just let him keep on riding. Finally they came to a group of cows with young calves, all needing a branding iron.

When Ricky turned to ride back, Jed asked him how large the ranch was.

"I've heard eight thousand acres, part of an old Spanish grant. Good title, too. I reckon Miss Ellen has a mortgage to worry about along with everything else."

"It's only a matter of time before some neighbor figures a way to steal some of these yearlings but they're not doing it yet because like you said, Ricky, they would show up too easy in somebody else's herd."

"What if someone was to buy a few head of Herefords, mix them with his Longhorns then start branding Miss Ellen's and mixing those in, too. Would anybody notice?"

"Not likely, Ricky and they'd probably figure Miss Ellen will fail anyway so they'd be just takin' from the bank or Artie Smith."

"Yeah, I guess you're right. She's been lucky so far. It ain't likely Artie's goin' to take kindly to you buying these few bulls, either. That's goin' to keep Miss Ellen in grub, at least for awhile."

"Well, Ricky, to tell the truth, I wouldn't mind meetin' up with this Artie Smith sometime before I head north."

"It's likely that's going to happen. Rolly says he rides over every couple of days. I expect you're goin' to want some sort of brand on them bulls before you leave and it's going to take a while sortin' out the best for breeders, put in a gather and put the brand to them."

"Is there a blacksmith forge at the ranch?"

"Yeah, sure and maybe there's still some coal around."

"Hope I can find a bit of iron laying about. I could put

Papa's own brand on right here if I could make an iron."

"Sure, there must be something, an old wagon rim or some such thing. I guess we should do that as soon as you make the deal with Miss Ellen."

When they were returning to the house, they could see another rider coming in from the Northwest. As they drew nearer, Ricky spoke up.

"Well, I guess you won't need to wait any longer to meet Mr. Artie Smith."

They rode into the ranch yard and saw Miss Ellen standing on the verandah and Artie Smith was about to step down from the saddle.

As he touched ground, Jed rode right up beside him.

"I take it you're Artie Smith?"

"That's right and you're that long drink of water that thinks he's gonna ship some bulls to Wyoming. I'll tell you right now stay on that horse and head him North. There ain't nothin' here for you. Anything around here that looks good is already got a claim stake, so git."

"I don't reckon I will. Now, me and Miss Ellen, we have business to discuss so get back up there on your horse and ride. You ain't welcome here."

Artie reached up and grabbed Jed's arm to yank him from the saddle but before he could get a good pull, Jed just dove head first, taking Artie Smith right under the feet of Smith's horse. Luckily, the horse danced sideways without doing either of them any damage. Jed untangled himself and jumped to his feet.

Artie Smith was a big man, not as tall as Jed but heavier by forty pounds and not too much fat.

Jed waited till Artie came to his feet then slapped him open handed on the jaw and stepped back. Artie just did what he figured. He put his head down between his shoulders and charged. Jed side stepped and belted him in the windpipe with his right hand. Artie doubled over and before he could straighten, Jed hit him with a right to the chin. Artie went over on his back and stayed down. After a few seconds, he rolled over and came to his knees. From that position, he looked up at Jed.

"Mister, you just signed your death warrant. Nobody does that to Artie Smith. You meet me in front of the livery in town tomorrow noon or leave the country."

"Well, I guess I could make time for that. I take it you're talkin' guns. Now, climb on your horse and go and don't show your face here again."

Artie Smith dragged himself into the saddle and rode away. It was then Jed realized his right hand was paining and when he looked, it was already swelling. Not a good start to a gunfight!

Miss Ellen noticed his hand, too.

"Mr. Owens, your hand! Come inside and soak it before it gets any worse. Goodness, you're not serious about meeting him tomorrow with guns. Anyway, you can't possibly draw a gun with that hand."

Miss Ellen informed them all that lunch was ready and that she had just come to the door to see if they were back yet when Artie Smith rode in.

In the kitchen, she got a basin of water and added some salt and set it so Jed could soak his hand. As she was wondering how Jed would feed himself, he picked up his fork and speared a slice of bread and then some bacon, slid a couple of eggs onto his plate and started eating left handed.

"Oh, I see you're left handed. You can draw with your left hand."

"Well, to tell the truth, Miss Ellen, I'm neither left nor right. I can do what I need to do with either hand. For most things my hands are equal. I always carried a gun on my right but I can shoot left handed. Even did a bit of two gun practise when I was younger out where nobody could see. Most folks have seen me do some one thing left handed and might find it strange but I can do everything with my left that I can with my right. Equally important, I do all left handed things with my right. But you are correct, I'm at a disadvantage. I don't have a left hand holster with me. Would there be a saddle maker in the area?"

"Sure, old man Estey does some work. He still has his shop in Breckenridge."

"Ricky, do you suppose you could get him to make me a left hand holster before tomorrow at eleven o'clock?"

"Sure. I might have to tell him why you need it. That will get him started. Ain't many around here care for Artie Smith."

"Well, somebody likes him or at least is on his payroll. He knew I'd be shipping bulls. The only one I can think of would be that agent at the station. Guess we might as well get this business over with before we start gathering and branding. I suppose I might as well get the branding iron made in town, means I have to go there anyway."

"I could get that done in Breckenridge, too. Ike Winslow has a forge and does some work. You give me a drawing of what you want and I'll get it."

After lunch, Jed got his gun and holster out of the bed roll and gave it to Ricky.

"Tell the man to make it like this right hand one, only opposite and make it fit the gun proper. Now, if I had some paper and pencil, I'd draw what the *Rocking O* looks like. It's just what it sounds like but it should be close in size. Here's some money and here's your wages. You sure came through on your end."

"I'm not so sure I did you a favour but I surely did want to help Miss Ellen if I could. Well, I best get started. I'll leave you with Miss Ellen to get the business part over with."

"Are you sure you don't want to head back home, Mr. Owens? Seems like you're getting in for a lot of trouble."

"No, Miss Ellen, I came for breed bulls and by golly, I'm goin' to get them. As you know, I'll be picking the most likely young ones so I expect to pay a premium for that but I've got no idea what I should be paying."

"While you were out riding with Ricky, I asked Rolly what I might get for them. It's pretty hard for me to know, being as how we haven't shipped for over a year. He said for yearling steers shipped for beef, we get around forty dollars a head. I guess if you was to take the best, you'll probably get mostly stuff that's fifteen months and the most likely of the lot so I guess I should get maybe sixty dollars each. Does that sound about right?"

"Well, Miss Ellen, I guess we've got a deal. I'll not pay less than sixty and we'll see how good they look when we get the lot cut out. Maybe I can go a might higher."

"You've seen my dog outside, I guess. Take him when you go to work the cattle, he's good and he loves it. Ricky knows how to work him and maybe I'll ride some myself. I expect if you're going to get the twelve best, we'll see every critter on the ranch before it's over. Maybe that might be a good thing. The cattle have been on their own pretty much for four months now."

"I'm quite sure I'm going to need help with the cattle. Do you know of anyone that I could hire to help Ricky?"

"I know Chad Watson is somewhere around and as soon as he hears that you're bucking Artie Smith, I expect he'll pay us a call."

"Well, I'm going in to Richardson now. This hand is surely givin' me trouble. Maybe I ought to see a doctor. I might have a bone broken. This hand of mine won't be much use for a while but I'll be able to ride and spot the ones I want. That's about all."

Jed hadn't unsaddled after looking for the steers so he mounted up and headed for Richardson. He didn't know the area very well but he took a shortcut past Breckenridge. He reached Richardson in time to see the doctor and then have supper. He didn't think his hand was broken but he had a notion that Artie Smith might back out of their meeting tomorrow unless he was to think he had a handicap.

At that moment, Artie was telling Dave, his foreman about this meeting coming up tomorrow.

"But Boss, you don't know anything about this Owens. He might be a second Wild Bill Hickock."

"Ain't I the best gun man around here?"

"Yes, Boss but he ain't from around here. He's from north of Cheyenne somewhere. Those boys up there might still be shooting each other seven days a week. I think you spoke a little too hasty."

"Well, it's too late now. I can't show yeller."

"How about if it was arranged for the Marshall to break it up? That way no one could say you backed out and you know he hates gun play in the streets."

"I think you've got it right. You go get the Marshall at just the right time and I'll wait till I see Herb comin' before I step out."

Just then his stable hand came running in.

"I just saw that guy you fought with. I'm sure it was him. He just came out of Doc Fraser's with his hand all bandaged."

"Which hand?"

"His right."

"There now, we'll have to make a new plan! We'll have to get the Marshall away somewhere. This is too good a chance to pass up."

"Good thing you have a hard head, Boss. He must of busted his hand this afternoon on your jaw."

"Well, after tomorrow, we'll be rid of the Wyoming Kid. Then we're going to think of something to finish off Miss Ellen Pritchard."

After Artie got up to the house, he poured himself a good drink and sat down in his chair. First, he went back over the afternoon out at the Pritchard place. He knew he had come up a might short but tomorrow he'd make up for that. Then the thought came that this Jed Owens was maybe left handed.

He went over the scene as it had played out. The first thing that came to mind was the saddle rope. It was on the right side. That pretty well clinched it. Then there was the fight itself. He'd got hit in the windpipe twice with an uppercut. Both were from the right he was sure and when he rushed Owens, Owens had stepped aside so he could hit with his right hand.

No doubt Owens would be a no show. Oh, well, if he didn't show, he'd make sure that the boys told the story around and leave out the fact that Owens had a broken right hand.

After Jed left the doctors office, he went to the Last Chance and had a drink, fumbling with his left hand to get the glass to his mouth. Then he went to the Cafe across the street for supper. He spent at least an hour trying awkwardly to corner some peas on his plate.

Deciding he had play acted long enough, he left the Cafe and rode back to the Pritchard ranch. The Doctor hadn't wanted to bandage his hand, said it was only sprained but Jed had insisted, saying he had some rough work to do and he just didn't want to injure it further.

Ricky was back in the bunkhouse and had brought Chad Watson with him. Chad had heard that someone at the Pritchard spread was digging their heels in to help Miss Ellen and he wanted to take a hand. Everyone was still up trying to catch up on everything that happened that day.

Ricky reported that he had success at the saddle makers and with the blacksmith.

"Old man Estey wanted to be contrary but when I told him

why we needed it, he went right to work. Said he'd make you the best dang holster you ever saw. And Ike Winslow, he was just waitin' for something to do. Said his forge had been cold for days."

"Well, we've done good today, boys so I think I'll turn in."

Rolly told them he'd report up to the house before he turned in. Miss Ellen wouldn't sleep unless she knew they were alright.

Chapter 4

The next morning at breakfast, everyone seemed tensed up, except Jed. Especially Miss Ellen.

"Maybe he won't show."

"Oh, I'm sure he'll show up. I made sure enough people saw me with my hand bandaged. He'll get the word and he's the kind to take the advantage if he thinks he has one."

"But why bring this gunfight on if it needn't take place? Anything could happen."

Well, the way I see it, if this continues, you get two choices ... walk away and let him get the ranch on a mortgage sale or fight to keep it."

"If you walk away, no one will get hurt."

"Ricky and Chad have already been beaten up. If you plan to fight, someone will likely get killed, possibly me sometime before we get those bulls ready to ship. Somewhere from ambush, most likely. This way, I'll have my chance and it's a good chance to deal Artie Smith out of the game. He probably won't be killed. I don't think he's the type that will keep on fighting after he's hit. If he's only laid up for a month, it should give you time to ship some cattle and get all the rest of the work caught up around here. You can take what money you get from me and hire enough men to get things in good shape."

"But when he recovers, he'll come at me all the more. He

39

held back before because he wanted me and the ranch. Now he'll settle for the ranch."

"I've some ideas about that but we'll talk later. Right now, I'd better get started for town."

Jed stopped at the saddle shop in Breckenridge and then the blacksmith shop. Both places had the work done and waiting.

Old man Estey gave Jed a warning that Artie Smith would try anything to get an advantage and for Jed to watch his eyes for tricks.

He had plenty of time till noon so he went to the Cafe and had coffee and pie. The place was empty so Sally took the time to find out what was going on. Jed told her about the coming dual in Richardson.

"I'm surprised the Marshall would stand for that. Not that he's such a great Marshall but he likes to keep things quiet around town. I guess gun shots wake him up. I haven't heard of a shooting in town for ages."

"I won't go against the Marshall if he steps in but I have a suspicion Mr. Smith will find something to keep the Marshall busy. I made it rather obvious that I couldn't pull a gun with my right hand and he'll want to see me back down or kill me. Either way, he would again have the upper hand. Right now, I have some people backing my play but if Artie should win today, that will disappear like smoke."

"I hope for your sake and Miss Ellen's that everything works out."

On his ride to Richardson, Jed went over his strategy in his head. He decided it would be best if he arrived suddenly right at noon. Let Smith relax and think he had backed out. Work on his nerves.

Maybe Artie would back down but he doubted that would happen. Most likely, he would know by now that Jed's right hand was in a big bandage.

Also, by showing up at the last minute, Smith wouldn't know about his left handed holster. By then it would be too late for Smith to back down and have any credibility with his crew.

Artie Smith, on the other hand had no notion of backing down. He was making plans to keep the Marshall from interfering.

"Dave, you go to the west end of town and at five minutes to twelve, you fire two shots then skedaddle and don't let anyone see you.

"Mike, you be close to the Marshall's office in case he don't hear Dave's shots. You run in and tell him you heard two shots at the far end of town. Maybe he's heard about this comin' shootout and if he has, he'll figure it's taking place at the west end. By the time he talks to some people to see what they know, the whole thing will be over. If Owens shows up, that is."

"I gotta hand it to you, Artie, your plan will work and I'm sure we'll have enough bystanders to witness the shootin' to clear you with the Marshal when he shows up. Why do you suppose Owens showed up here last night with that bandaged hand?"

"Maybe just to get the public on his side when he backs down, most likely. I can't think of anything else."

"Well, Boss, make sure you go first. Every second counts. I sure hope you know what you're doin'."

"What could go wrong? I went over everything from yesterday. He's right handed. Now his right hand is useless. If I can't beat him now, I might as well step aside and let him do whatever he wants out at the Pritchard place."

"From what I heard around town, he's only here to buy some bulls to ship north. He'd be gone in a couple of days. He can't make much difference."

41

"He's already made a difference. That Ricky Danson came to town with him, from where I don't know. The next thing you know, they'll start a gather for shipment. If they get that done, that woman will hang on for another year. If I could get the damn bank to foreclose, this thing would be over but Amos, over at the Cattleman's Bank, he just says there's no hurry, that there's plenty out there to cover the mortgage. I never seen him be that easy on anyone before. Maybe he has a soft spot for women that we don't know about.

"Well, it's twenty minutes to twelve. Dave, you better get to the west side and find a place where you can fire two shots and get away without bein' seen."

"I know just the place and maybe I can get back here to watch. What about you, Mike?"

"I guess maybe I can slip away from the Marshall. Good luck, Boss."

Jed rode to the backside of the livery and tied his horse to the corral fence. At least if he got killed, the horse would be home.

He entered through the back door and made his way to the front. The livery man was lounging in a chair just outside. Jed stopped within the barn's shadow and spoke.

The livery man jumped and almost went over backwards. When he got his bearings, he looked around. Oh, it's you. Was that horse alright?"

"Sure, just fine. But I'll need him for awhile yet though. I just tied him to the corral out back."

"Okay. You stay here for awhile. Maybe you'll have a ringside seat for some gun play. Artie Smith challenged some stranger to meet him here at twelve o'clock. I thought that sort of thing was past. Haven't heard of a shootin' here about's for years. I hear tell Artie Smith is pretty salty. At least that's what he tells folks. Moved here about five years ago so no one knows much about him. There's a story goin' that this stranger has a busted hand. Hit Artie in the jaw yesterday, they say. Should of known better than to hit a bone head like that with his fist."

The livery man started to light his pipe but couldn't find a match so he turned to Jed.

"You got a match? This old chair is gettin' so comfortable, I don't want to get up."

When Jed started rummaging for a match with his left hand, the livery man noticed the bandage.

"Well, gosh and be darned, you're the man Artie's gunning for. You gonna meet him with a hand like that?"

"It's either that or leave town without what I came for."

"With your hand bandaged like that, you ain't likely gonna leave town ever."

"I still have one good hand."

I ain't never seen a man that was much good left handed. With most of them two gun men years back, that left hand gun was just for back up. If I was you, I'd skedaddle out that back door and ride."

"No, I think I'll stay right here. I expect Mr. Smith to show in a couple of minutes. Somehow, he'll keep the Marshall out of it. I don't know how but he'll think of something. He'll think like you that he has the advantage. It's not just that I hit him yesterday. I'm gettin' in his way out at the Pritchard ranch."

"Well, yes, I've heard Artie's been makin' brags that he'd expand his horse ranch out there. At one time, he had his eye on Miss Ellen but I think he's given up on that."

"Do you mind if I stay here in the shade for the next few minutes?"

"I'd be obliged if you would but leave me out of the line of fire when the time comes. I'm going to stay right here in my chair and watch the last gunfight of the century, no doubt. The last one in this town at least. Now you watch Artie. I expect he'll try something tricky."

Just then they heard two shots on the west side of town.

"Well, dang-it all. Somebody's already shootin' it up over something."

"I guess that would be Artie's decoy to pull the Marshall out of the way. Now that he knows I've got a bad hand, he wants this thing to go through. If the Marshall has gotten word of this shootin', he most likely will figure it's already taking place. I give Artie about two more minutes then he'll be here. He's probably told folks I'll not show. I'll let him have his day in the sun before I step out."

"You any good with that dang left handed rig?"

"Well, I'm almost as good as with my right. The only thing is, I don't know how good Mr. Smith might be. Haven't ever seen him draw and shoot."

"No, I never did, either. Heard stories but they were probably started by Artie himself. Yep, you were right. Here comes Artie now. Still two minutes by this old turnip of mine and it's usually about right."

"You keep an eye on your watch and tell me when it hits high noon."

Just as it turned high noon, Artie turned to someone on the side walk.

"See, I knew it would be a no show. Hit me yesterday when I weren't looking but he ain't got the guts to meet my challenge."

While Artie was talking, Jed stepped out in the bright sun and to the side by three or four steps. Artie noticed his listener look across the street toward the livery. He turned and saw Jed.

"I see you finally got here."

"I've been here for ten minutes listening to you brag. Now it's noon so lets get on with it."

Artie was taken aback. He had himself set to go to the Last Chance, belly up to the bar and brag. Yet, he could see that Owens had a bandage on his right hand but he had his gun on the left. No one he'd ever heard of could draw and shoot straight left handed.

Yet this Owens seemed confident. He was about ready to back down when Dave arrived and hollered, "Take him, Artie," and he automatically started his draw.

His gun came out. He knew that he was going to get this skinny beanpole. Then his whole right side went numb. Everything went black and he fell on his side. People started running forward and surrounding Artie.

"Dang it," somebody said. "He's still alive. Shoot him again, stranger."

Just then Marshall Herb Peels arrived, all out of wind.

"Let me through there. What in Sam Hill's going on in this town today. Gunshots everywhere."

"Well, Marshall, I'll tell you what went on here. Artie Smith called out the wrong man. Looks like he might live though if we could get him to the Docs place before he bleeds out."

"Some of you boys get something to carry him on and take him there. The rest of you stay here. I need to know what took place."

"There ain't much to tell, Marshall. Artie had a fallin' out with Mr. Owens yesterday and then challenged him to meet him with a gun here today."

"I heard a rumour that Artie had something goin' but then those dang shots west of here took me out that way. Couldn't find out what that was about."

"Well, Marshall, I reckon that was Artie gettin' you out of the way."

"Where's this Mr. Owens? How come he hasn't stepped forward to explain himself?"

"As soon as he fired, he stepped back into the shadows of the barn. I guess he figured maybe Artie had some help posted somewhere."

"Well, I'm going to get to the bottom of this. I don't like

gun fights here in town."

As the Marshall approached the barn, Jed stepped out.

"You the one that shot Artie?"

"Yep."

"Well, give me your gun and come on down to the office."

"I'll come to the office but I'll give you my gun when I get there."

"You figure he might have a sniper?"

"If I was you, I wouldn't walk too close going down the street."

"Come along. Maybe we can get to the bottom of this."

"Just ask the people outside who started his draw first."

"I'll be asking these people some questions alright but first I want your story, why you're in my town shooting down the citizens."

As soon as they entered the Marshall's office, Jed took off the gun belt and laid it on the Marshall's desk.

"First thing I want to know is how come you're in my area. Rumour has it you're from up north a fair piece. How could you and Artie Smith get to be pullin' iron so quick. You know this Artie Smith from somewhere before?"

"Never saw the man till yesterday."

"How come you're shootin' him today?"

"Well, I'd better start with why I came to town. We needed some Hereford bulls and I left home heading this way to find them.

"I came all the way to Amarillo before I heard that a ranch outside of town here had some young stuff that hadn't been cut. I rode out there yesterday morning and sure enough, they had just what I needed but this Artie Smith came ridin' in like he owned the place, pulled me off my horse and meant to beat the crap out of me. I managed to get in a few good licks and it was over. Neither one of us was armed but Mr. Smith challenged me to meet him here today at noon. I busted my hand on Mr. Smith's jaw so I got a left hand holster made."

"And you beat Artie left handed?"

"Most folks don't know it but some people can do chores with either hand."

"You sure did a job on Artie. Now I ain't lockin' you up but you stay here till I talk to some of them witnesses. I suppose I'll have to write everything down. I hate paperwork."

"Sorry to have put you to the bother, Marshall. I'll just sit here till you get back."

An hour later, the Marshall came back.

"They tell me Artie made his brags that he challenged you to a shootout and that he went for his gun first so there's no point in me holding you.

"Doc says Artie might live if there's no complications though he'll probably not have much use of that arm. Seems your shot busted the shoulder joint. Doc says the bones will probably knit together and he'll only have movement at the elbow. I guess he's been givin' trouble to Miss Pritchard. I didn't know that. My duties only cover the town.

"If you have any more shootin' to do, do it outside of town limits. I'll have to write two dang pages of notes in case Artie disagrees with you later. Here's your gun belt. You're free to go."

As soon as Artie was shot, Dave and Mike got together to decide what to do.

"Dave, what are you figurin'?"

"Artie might not make it and if he does, he won't have much standing in this town. I can't see you nurse maiding him for the rest of your life."

"I'm thinkin' you and me should ride right back to the ranch and pack up. I don't think I'll be too careful what I pack. By tomorrow, somebody will be lookin' to see about the horses and who should be overseer for Artie."

"I'm for that. I'm thinkin' I'll head north for a spell, ain't no one knows me up there. Let's go."

By the time Jed got back to the livery, there was a crowd gathered around the old livery man listening to his story, much embellished most likely but Jed didn't stop. He picked up his horse and headed straight away for the Pritchard ranch. The folks there would be worrying about what happened and there was no reason to keep Miss Ellen waiting.

As he rode into the ranch yard, Rolly, Ricky and Chad were all there sitting on the verandah. Old Rolly was the first to speak.

"Well, did he show?"

"Yep, he showed."

"Well, what happened?"

"Gosh dang it all, tell us about it! Don't keep me asking questions."

"Artie Smith is at the doctor's house, touch and go they say. A bullet wound in the right shoulder. If he lives it ain't likely he'll have use of his shoulder joint so he won't bully anyone again. Not even women."

"It ain't likely he'll hang around when he heals up. Them boys of his will take what they can pack off this very night. Just wait and see."

"Where's Miss Ellen? I been wantin' to tell her she can get that branding done and ship whatever she needs to, except those bulls. I've got an idea she could do better putting them up for auction right in town. Advertise in the Cattleman's Paper across Texas."

"Miss Ellen ain't been feelin' proper since you left here this morning. Fact is, me and the boys had to get our own lunch. Seems she thinks she should have done something to stop you. I told her there weren't nothing could stop you. You gave Artie Smith your word you'd be there and I figured your word was good."

"I'd best go in and show her I'm still in one piece or you boys will be tryin' to cook supper."

Everybody stayed right where they were and just watched Jed go through the door. Then old Rolly grinned.

"Cool customer, ain't he?"

"I bet he'll be a bit flustered before Miss Ellen gets done with him."

"What do you bet she's doin' about now?"

"I figure it's fifty-fifty ... either she's in his arms crying her eyes out or she's giving him a piece of her tongue for taking such a chance."

"I don't hear no voices so I guess he's gettin' the soft treatment."

"Well, Rolly, I'm bettin' we're going to have a new boss man around here within a few days. Tough one, too. Might even make you get off your butt."

"If that's what it takes to get this place going, I'll give it my best."

"One thing's for sure, he's gonna want those bulls shipped as soon as possible. He's been on the road for a month now, stopping every fifty miles and askin' everyone about Herefords. Lucky I ran into him in Amarillo. I think he was about ready to turn back."

"There is one thing that we ain't talked about, Ricky. It's that dang mortgage. It ain't had a payment for nigh on eight months, I figure. I don't know how come something ain't been done before this. I know for a fact Miss Ellen tried for more money before she let you boys go. I guess the bank figured they'd wait and see, not wantin' to force the issue for more property than the mortgage was worth. Miss Ellen, she told me one time she owed ten thousand plus interest. Her Pa borrowed to get started with these Herefords."

Ten minutes later, Miss Ellen and Jed came out the door with Jed looking a bit flustered and Miss Ellen's face having turned from a ghostly white to a certain shade of red.

"Rolly, Chad, Ricky ... I want you to know you're back on the payroll. Mr. Owens will be foreman for the next little while so you take orders from him. If you know any men around town needing work, you ride right now and get them. Up to six men, Jed tells me."

"Well, Miss Ellen, this ain't the busiest time of year so I guess the best thing we could do is ride to the neighbours. I'm sure some of them would be glad to lighten their payroll for a month."

"You boys decide who and what we need. Rolly, tomorrow you hitch up the buckboard. There isn't enough food in this house to make a decent supper. That's all I've got to say. From now on, it's Mr. Owens you take orders from. He isn't familiar with the ranch so I expect you boys to be as helpful as you can."

Miss Ellen went back inside and the boys all turned to Jed with a smirk on their faces.

Ricky said, "I guess us boys know why Miss Ellen was so upset that we had to cook up our own lunch."

Jed's face turned red again.

"She's a right nice lady and I reckon she feels a might responsible for our welfare."

"Yeh," Rolly said, "especially one long, lanky dude from Wyoming."

"Stop your joshing, boys. She's only known me for two days."

"Time don't mean nothin' to a female. Now and again they can be right notional. Now, don't you go and break her heart. Us boys set great store by that Miss."

"Let's get down to business, boys. Is there time left before dark to see about a few extra hands?"

"Sure. We could ride to two, maybe three places and ask around."

"Okay then, be on your way. I'd like to have this gather

and branding started before I have to head north. I don't expect that will be more than three days."

After Ricky and Chad rode out, Jed turned his horse into the corral and forked in some hay then came back to the verandah and sat down next to Rolly. One thing he'd noticed about these old semi-retired cowboys, they always felt they needed to do something to earn their keep. If they couldn't ride any more they would try to make it up in other ways. Providing information was one way.

"Rolly, if you were me and takin' twelve young bulls on a five or six day train ride, what would you do? I've never rode the cars before."

"Well, I'll tell you, Jed, I have ... many times, all the way to Chicago. Can't do it anymore though or I'd go with you."

"Did you feed on the fly when you were going and what about water?"

"You got to have some feed. Most times stock won't eat as much when their moving. Course if you lay over somewhere then they'll sure eat. Cattle cars have a water tank but it won't last you six days. Not in hot weather. Maybe five with just twelve critters. Mostly we'd get to Chicago in three or four days and sometimes them critters were pretty dry by that time. If you don't get laid over on a siding waitin' for a train back to Cheyenne, you should be alright for water. If you need water, you'll have to bribe the engineer to pull you up to the water tank. Sure wish I could go with you."

"I need you here, Rolly. Just look after Miss Ellen like you have been. I'm going to leave Ricky in charge while I'm gone."

"I guess you're comin' back then?"

"Oh, sure but I might be gone for two or three weeks, depending on what might be going on at the *Rocking O*."

Chapter 5

The next morning, Jed rode with Ricky to the first bunch of cattle. They were mostly yearlings.

"What are we going to do with these yearlings as we catch them. We can't start a fire every time we find a critter you want."

"I'm thinking we should take them one by one to the horse corral. We can move the horses out and picket them at night. When we get what bulls we want, we'll brand them. I can't throw a rope worth a dang but I could lead them in to the corral after you or Chad get a rope on them"

"Okay, we'll see how it goes. Sometime this mornin', we should have help ... three, maybe four local boys will show up I think. When word gets around, we might get more. What's your idea for the rest of them?"

"I'm thinkin' Miss Ellen should be getting a herd ready and shipped right away. So we need a gather done and all the unbranded stock needs to be looked at, too. The agent told us the other day that cattle traffic was way down this time of year so there shouldn't be a problem finding cars."

"How many days you figuring on being here?"

"Not more than three after today. I've already been gone nearly four weeks."

"Then you're comin' back?"

"Yep. Rolly asked that same thing last night. Miss Ellen would like for me to ramrod this outfit into shape and I agreed to help her. While I'm gone, I'm going to leave it in your hands. If anything happens that I need to know about, send a telegram to Cheyenne. I'll check there whenever I can. My father's got some problems he's trying to sort out while I'm away and hopefully the smoke will be settled by the time I get home.

"Rolly says I'm probably going to be five or six days gettin' to Cheyenne, seeing as I've got to go east first and then back west, depending on some west bound train pickin' me up at a siding."

"Sounds about right."

"There's one nice bull, probably fifteen months old. That will be the start. Look at that dog go. He must have read my mind. He's already movin' him out."

"Yep, he watches all the time. When you nodded your head at that critter, he knew what you wanted and he's ready to work. Hasn't had any herdin' to do unless you count followin' Rolly around the yard."

"Let's get a rope on him and I'll lead him in to the corral. That's about all I can do with this hand of mine."

"Before you do that, see if there's another in this bunch. If there is, me and the dog will catch it and meet you halfway. Then we'll look up the next bunch. It's likely we'll get most of them today by the last trip in. We can each take one at lunch time."

By nightfall, they had twelve very nice bulls, eight and nine hundred pounds each ... solid, all muscle. Three men showed up throughout the day and Jed put them to work at various chores, everything from fixing things around the ranch to cleaning out water holes.

Tomorrow, they'd start the gather of the rest of the young cattle and start branding. The new calves wouldn't be a problem but those Hereford yearlings would fight the rope. It would take two men, one to get a rope around the neck and one to rope the hind feet.

He'd help them for one day. Then he had to brand those bulls and then go to town and see about a rail car and feed.

One other thing he had to think about was what to do about Miss Ellen and himself. It was true he could be a big help to her getting the ranch back on a paying basis yet it was something any good foreman could do. Ricky could do it if he had a bit more confidence in himself. Anyway, he had promised to come back so he'd better keep himself in line till then.

By the time he got back, things would be straightened out here. Maybe Miss Ellen wouldn't look at him in the same way she was now which was kind of nice he had to admit but until he had something to put in the pot, he'd better not think of dealing himself into a game like that. Not only would people look at him funny, he'd also be soul searching for the rest of his life. Better to keep those thoughts at arms length and let the coming separation sort things out.

When he did the branding of the bulls, he used the whole crew. They were big, strong animals and he didn't want anyone getting hurt. They'd throw each one then put a blanket over it's head with a man to hold the head down. They still fought but they couldn't see what was taking place at their flank and with a red hot branding iron, it only took a second or two to get a good mark on them.

Tomorrow, he had to go to town. He'd been putting it off for two days. He liked the feel of being in charge, getting things done and seeing the difference every night. At the *Rocking O,* he had achieved a great deal but he had to do it in a round about way. And every time he did something his own way, he had trouble with John.

Papa was right. It was time he left the *Rocking O*. There was no way Papa would break his word to his grandfather and there was no way he and John could live on the same ranch. Maybe John would make the decisions if Jed wasn't around. Maybe he had the stuff to make the ranch pay but Jed had his doubts.

One thing was sure, if John did anything to Del and Rose while he was gone, there was going to be a dust up when he got back.

The next morning, he rode into town and left his horse at the livery. The hostler wanted to talk about the shoot out but Jed told him he didn't want to talk about it. It was something to forget.

He made his way to the train station, noting that there were cattle cars on the siding. Maybe he was in luck.

The same agent was on duty as the day he had arrived from Abilene. He remembered that this man had probably told Artie Smith his business but he decided he wouldn't get what he wanted by confronting him. Anyway, Artie Smith wouldn't be paying any more bribes or buying drinks for awhile.

"I see you have some cattle cars on the siding."

"Oh, sure. It's the slack time so the company parks them wherever they'll be out of the way till fall."

"I suppose I could book one of those cars to take my bulls to Cheyenne?"

"Oh, sure but it'll cost and we don't have any hay here right now. Later on, the company will bring in some pressed hay from back east then you cattlemen can buy what you need. Right now though, we don't have not one bale."

"Would you mind if I look inside one of those cars?"

"I guess you could but I'll have to go with you. The cars are all locked up. Can't have kids playing in there. All that chaff and bits of hay ... good chance they'd have the whole works on fire."

Inside, the boxcar was open except for a four foot isle

straight across from side to side. It looked like he might put the twelve young bulls in one end and use the other for loose hay, if he could find some.

Another thing he would need would be food for himself. Some cans, jerky and hardtack, he supposed. There would be no fires so he'd have to go without coffee.

When they got back up to the station, the agent enquired did he want to book a car.

"Well, I'll have to find some hay first then I'll let you know. Would the railroad bring some hay out if there was, say a hundred and fifty head to ship?

"I reckon I could check. Who's planning on shippin' right now? Never knowed anyone to ship beef in the summer."

"The Pritchard ranch is makin' a gather but don't tell Artie Smith about that. It could set him back knowing he can't do anything about it."

After Jed left the station, he went to the livery stable to find out where they got their hay.

"I buy mine from Ed Curtis. He lives just up the valley here, maybe three miles. Just loose hay, mind you. He should be gettin' a new cut about now, I'd say. You can ride out and see him. I'm sure he'd love to get some business."

When he arrived at the Curtis place, sure enough it was hay making time so he rode right into the field. There was a man on the ground he assumed was Ed Curtis and a boy of about fourteen building a load up top on a hay rack on a huge wagon.

Jed got right down to business.

"I hear you've got hay for sale."

"Yep."

"How much?"

"How much money for how much hay?"

"How about a wagon load. Would that fill half of a cattle car?"

56

"Sure but what's wrong with their baled hay?"

"They don't have any this time of year. Ain't no call for it the agent says and I can't wait for them to send some out from wherever they ship it from."

"So you need a wagon load right now?"

"No, day after tomorrow. First thing in the morning."

"How much you paying?"

"Well, I figure whatever you charge the livery stable."

"Cash on delivery?"

"Sure."

"Then I'll save my last load. I'll just back the wagon into the barn and hitch it up come day after tomorrow. Should be there by seven-thirty."

"Then I'll see you there."

On his way back to town, he realized he would need a hay fork and a bucket on board. He'd have to stop at the store in town and purchase them. And he was running short of money. There was some extra in that twelve hundred dollar bank draft. More than enough to pay for the bulls, he'd better stop at the Wells Fargo Bank and cash it.

After that he went back to the station and signed for the rail car and asked when he might expect to get started if he loaded day after tomorrow. Early afternoon, he was told. There would be a train coming from the west in the afternoon and if they had the capacity, they would hook on and take him east.

"Most times, we have entire trains with nothing but cattle. They were assigned their own engine and crew."

But Jed would have to take whatever circumstance offered.

"What's it going to cost me. Can you tell me that?"

"Not till I check the mileage but I'd say between three and four hundred dollars. That's payable at this end before you load."

"What do these ranchers do when they ship to Chicago? Do they have to pay before they load?"

"Nope. They sell to a cattle buyer and they're all bonded to the railroad. The tariff is guaranteed, you see."

"Any buyers in town right now?"

"Nope. Might be one or two in Abilene."

"How could I find out?"

"Send a telegram to Abilene. The buyers have a thing with the agents. They'll get the message."

"Okay. I'd like to send a message. Just say two hundred mixed Herefords, ready to load, seven days."

"This Miss Ellen's herd?"

"Yes, they're doing the gather now so they should be ready for a buyer to see by the time he can get here from Abilene and then the buyer will have to arrange for hay. So I guess he'll need at least a week."

"Yes, maybe longer."

"Well, I've signed for the car so get the bill ready for me when we bring those bulls in. It won't take long to load so I'll wait till morning, day after tomorrow. Got hay coming then. What about the water tank, how do I get that filled?"

"Well, I guess the train crew will have to take the time to pull your car by the water tower and fill it before they pull out."

When he was riding back to the ranch, he was thinking about all the things he had to look after and whether he'd left anything out. One thing for sure, he was going to be short of money before he got home.

At supper that night, he explained about the rail cars and what he'd done about getting a buyer.

"Well, dang," Rolly said, "I never thought any other time there would be buyers nosin' around but this time of year I suppose they are in Abilene. Makes sense."

"Well, let's hope someone shows up before we get this

gather done."

"You won't be here to talk to the buyer. What you reckon we should get straight across the board?"

"I really don't know. All you can do is look at the prices you got last time and try to get at least what you got then. I think Miss Ellen should have a say in what price she takes. Don't sell too cheap. Don't sell those young bulls with the rest. If he wants them, ask within ten dollars of what I'm payin' for mine, considering I picked the best."

Two days later, the bulls were loaded and the hay was in place. He had what food he figured he could stow and keep for six days. Now he had to wait for an east bound freight and he mustn't forget that he needed that water tank filled.

He took his horse back to the livery and paid his bill. He had fifty dollars left and he wouldn't have had that except Miss Ellen insisted he be paid for a week considering he rounded up and loaded his own cattle.

He hated to leave but there was no choice. He'd been sent here by his father to do this job and he had to stick to it till it was finished but this would be his last task for the *Rocking O* Ranch. There was no way to tell what the future held here in Texas but he would surely find out.

The young bulls were starting to get rowdy in their pen and he wished they were on the move. Once the train was moving, they would be busy keeping their balance. They wouldn't have time to act up.

In the meantime in another part of town, another man was waiting for that train to pull out.

Amos Mason, the manager of the Cattleman's Bank was studying the mortgage agreement of the Pritchard Ranch. He hadn't been manager at the time the mortgage was written up and he wasn't familiar with the terms. It seemed that the agreement was for a twelve thousand dollar loan to be used to stock the ranch with Hereford cattle. But the former manager had been shrewd enough to include all lands and cattle should the owner fail to make good on the loan. It was a year and a half since Joe Pritchard had died and since that time his daughter had paid just one payment. She was in arrears by twenty-five hundred dollars. The few dollars she would receive for those bulls would only go to pay the local merchants. The bank wouldn't get any of that.

He heard rumours that they were starting a gather and there was money coming in on deposit. Some buyer coming from Abilene. He had to make up his mind today whether to chance his scheme.

He'd have to take steps to foreclose and he needed the Judge to sign the papers and the Sheriff to serve them.

Once the bank had foreclosed, he would need an overseer to look after the place or there wouldn't be anything left. He knew without a doubt that local feelings would be running high, especially now that the Pritchard woman might make good.

Once the bank foreclosed, he could buy the place for the price of the mortgage plus a thousand dollars. He would have to put up mortgage sale notices he supposed but that could be done where no one would ever see them. The money he'd need, he could loan to himself right from the bank. As soon as the place was his, he'd find a buyer before anyone realized he owned it. Then he'd skip out. Maybe ask for a transfer and look for a similar opportunity elsewhere.

First he had to see that long drink of water that shot Artie Smith gone from town. He didn't know who he was but he had come all the way from Wyoming for twelve breeding bulls for a ranch called the *Rocking O*. There must be some money there and if he ever got wind of this little swindle, he might have the resources to stop it.

As soon as that cattle car left the siding, he'd have to get the Judge to sign the foreclosure form and find the county

Sheriff, wherever he might be. He and Herb Peels, the town Marshall weren't very buddy, buddy so he'd be no help there. The Sheriff could be any where in the county. His office wasn't even here in town. He'd have to send him a telegram and he wouldn't dare say too much. The quieter it was kept, the better. It had to be done before that buyer paid out money for those cattle. There wouldn't be enough to pay the mortgage off but if Miss Pritchard offered to pay a reasonable amount, the Judge or the Sheriff would put pressure to bear for him to accept it.

The Judge would insist that he give Miss Pritchard time to come up with the money but if he could get a clause in there to stop the sale or disposal of any and all assets covered by the mortgage that would mean she couldn't sell the cattle.

About two o'clock, he heard a train come in from the west and about three o'clock he heard it pull out. He could see the siding from his east window and when he looked, the cattle car was gone.

He gathered up all the paper work and left the office to locate the Judge which might take a while. It was a part time position for a retired District Attorney from somewhere back east. Judge Hendrick took that part time to mean whenever he felt like going to the office.

He finally left a note on the Judge's door informing him that he needed his signature on some important papers. He'd have to remember to ask the Judge where he might locate the Sheriff. Maybe the Judge would know if he was in the district, possibly serving papers or other work.

Chapter 6

Jed was having his first taste of riding a cattle car. He was right about the bulls. They stopped jousting and braced themselves against each other. They calmly rode the rails like they had done it all their lives.

Jed decided he might as well take a nap. The engineer had told him it would be at least five or six hours before the next stop. Then they'd need to refuel and take on water. He explained that freight trains had no scheduled stops and unless they had cars to drop off or pick up, they made do with just the stops for water.

The next time he woke, it was dark and they had stopped. He looked out through the slats on the side and he could see another set of tracks so he supposed they were pulled off to let a westbound go by. Just then he heard footsteps outside and then someone spoke.

"Hey, how you doin' in there?"

"I'm okay. Why are we stopped?"

"The westbound will be comin' through but there's no way of knowin' if she'll be on time. Might be an hour. You want some coffee? We got a pot on in the Caboose."

"Sure, that would be good. Might wake me up. I guess I slept four or five hours."

"Well, come along. Could even find a biscuit and some beef."

"Sounds good. All I brought was cans and some cold biscuits. Can't make coffee and don't want to drink the water from that cattle tank."

"Well, I can't blame you there. Probably hasn't had water in it since May. I'll give you a bottle and you fill it whenever we stop to tank up."

"I'm obliged. Let's get that coffee before that westbound comes by."

When they got to the door of the caboose, he could smell the coffee coming to a boil.

"That sure smells good. I thought I'd have to go without all the way to Cheyenne."

"Cheyenne? Aren't you going to Chicago?"

"No, I've got a load of Hereford bulls in there, taking them home for breeding."

"That makes sense. Lots of meat on those critters."

"Well, my father thinks so. Sent me out to find some and I travelled all the way to Richardson."

"Then you'll be leaving us where the tracks join. Another twenty four to thirty hours, if we don't have to stop like we are right now. Lucky you're next to the caboose. You're welcome to coffee any time we stop and help yourself to a biscuit and some roast beef. It ain't the best feed a man can have but it will keep you alive till you get something better. I'm Mike Gallagher, by the way. No known address, you might say. Just travel this old caboose from one side of the country to the other."

"I'm Jed Owens from the *Rocking O* Ranch just north and west of Cheyenne, only address I've ever had with generations of Owens on the same spot. Well, I'm going to leave you. I've got to pitch some hay to those critters. I don't want my lantern burning while we travel. A jolt could set it flying into that hay pile."

"I'm glad you're safety conscious. Some of these cowboys that ride the cattle cars are drunk all the way to Chicago."

"Well, I hope I can get some more sleep. Sure makes the time fly."

The train made two more stops for water before they reached the track from Chicago.

The crew shunted his car onto an empty switch, waved goodby and pulled out for the east. Jed fed and watered the stock and then lay back in the hay. At least, he had a good bed and the stock seemed content to rest up from the trip. Mike Gallagher had informed him that he should have a shorter trip to Cheyenne than what he'd travelled so far.

He was starting to wonder now what was taking place back at the *Rocking O*. When he left, his father seemed to have something on his mind and he knew it was to do with the fight between himself and John.

He knew in his mind that things could not continue the way they were. John thought he should have all the say since he was to own the ranch someday but he was so contrary. He wanted to do everything his own way even when it was against the face of all reason.

It wasn't just Jed he fought with, it was their father, too. Right now, Jed was thinking he would head back to Texas as soon as he could get away. Let John try to run things on his own.

Their father had long since stopped trying to help John and he wondered why he had bothered with obtaining these bulls. Jed suspected it was just an idea Ben had come to at some time and he had used it to get Jed away from the ranch for a period of time.

Some way, Jed was determined to go back to Texas and the Pritchard Ranch. Miss Ellen needed a foreman and he was determined to be that man. She also needed financial help as well as labour. Somehow, if he had some money, he'd like to buy into an agreement with her. From what he had overheard, she had a mortgage and why the bank hadn't foreclosed, he couldn't understand. Anyway, if she got those cattle sold, she could get the mortgage paid up to date.

In the meantime, Amos Mason was trying his best to get the foreclosure notice on the Pritchard gate before that buyer arrived from Abilene and paid for the herd. If he arrived and saw those empty cars on the siding and a ready herd just seven miles outside of town, he might make the deal on the spot to keep someone else from getting ahead of him.

It was a risky scheme Amos had planned and if it didn't come off smoothly, he'd be in big trouble. He'd be using the banks money to buy what would be at the time a bank asset that would be worth close to forty thousand dollars and he would be buying it for about eleven thousand.

Still, if he could pull it off fast, he stood to make fifteen to twenty thousand in a short period, certainly before the next bank inspection. If it hadn't been for Artie Smith, he could have had it done two months ago. With Artie Smith watching every move, there was no way he could have gotten away with it.

That was one good thing the bull buyer had done for him by getting Artie Smith out of the way. But he had also gotten the outfit back working again. Branding and gathering a herd, even hired some hands off the neighbouring ranchers for temporary duty. Luckily, he was gone back north. According to what folks said, he got things done in a hurry.

If only he could have found the Judge this afternoon but he'd solve that problem tomorrow morning. He'd be on his door step before he could get away. Then there was the Sheriff. Lord knows how long it would take to contact him. It had better not be too long or his nerves would give out.

Jed had to wait till the next day to get his cattle car hitched to a freight going west. Before they pulled out, a passenger train passed them going west with a fancy Pullman car hitched next to the caboose. He supposed it was some railroad dignitaries. They didn't even stop for water. He guessed that with only a few light coaches to pull, they didn't use up water like a freight.

He was down to a third of a tank of water for the cattle but he decided he had enough to get to Cheyenne and he didn't want to ask the engineer to back his car down to the water tank to fill up.

Two days later, they pulled into Cheyenne. Five days total with the one day stopover so he should be able to get back to Richardson in four of five days if he could get the right connections.

They dropped off his car about four o'clock in the afternoon and Jed decided to get those young bulls out of their confined space as soon as possible. The first thing to do was to get his horse and gear from the livery. He'd have to find somewhere to leave the bulls overnight.

Maybe he could get some information at the livery. The hostlers talked to everyone who rode in or rode out. They seemed to be proud of all the gossip they picked up.

"Hello, Charlie."

"Well, Jed Owens. Didn't think you were ever comin' back. I sure did make use of your stock. Had a busy month since you left. Fact is, that pack horse is out right now but if you need one, I'll find you a mule or something."

"No, Charlie but I do need my saddle and maybe some information. Where can I leave twelve young bulls for overnight or even for a day or two?"

"You know, Jed, that's a funny thing, Ed Baker was saying today that it was such a bother to lead the town's milk cows way out to the country to be serviced. Lots of folks have just one or two cows for milking you know. No one has enough to keep a bull around. He was saying maybe some one should

get a good bull and charge for the service and here you come
along with twelve bulls."

"Do you know where I might put them, Charlie?"

"What I reckon we'll do is empty out that corral back there,
bring the two horses into the stall here and you can use the
corral. Providing maybe I could use one or two of those bulls
while they're here."

"Charlie, you've got a deal and I'll pay you for their care
while they're here."

"You leavin' for home tonight, Mr. Owens?"

"No. By the time I get those bulls into your corral, it will
be just about enough time to have supper and go to bed."

"Well, you get the saddle and gear on your horse there and
I'll go down the street and see if I can get you some help."

"Thanks, Charlie. I'll stand the drinks after."

By the time Jed rode out of the livery, there was a half
dozen men on horse back and a dozen towns people on foot,
all heading for the train station. It seemed Charlie had spun a
pretty good yarn.

When he got to the station, the ramp was already in place.
Jed opened the door and threw out what gear that travelled
with him and opened the pen. The bulls were ready to see the
outside and they came storming out but the men kept them
bunched and moving toward the livery corral.

"Charlie, you've sure done me right. The way those bulls
stormed out from that cattle car, I needed lots of help."

"I've already heard from two or three men that they need
bulls for their cows."

"If you want to make some money, Charlie, charge for the
service. Won't hurt the bulls any."

"No, Jed, not this time. But it's brought the idea to my head
that I could do it, if I could get me a nice gentle bull. I guess
one of those young ones could be gentled."

"No way, Charlie. I went half way across Texas to get

those. Although if I'd known your problem here in town, I could have brought an extra. There's still some loose hay in that car. I guess I should get a wagon and haul it up to the corral."

"I got a boy that helps me out some, I'll get him to do it. You go ahead and get your supper and find a room. This town sure is busy this summer. People travelling by stage and by rail and the ranchers don't seem to have nothin' to do except sleep in hotels and cozy up to the bar and gossip. Your Pa spent a week here in town right after you went south."

Jed headed for the Rancher's Roost and took a room for the night. When he went into the dining room, the place was full. Charlie was right.

After supper, he went to the livery stable again to get his gear in order and pay the boy for getting the hay out of the car. The lad was just unhitching the horse from the wagon.

"Mark just finished with the hay, Jed. Lots for a day, anyway. How long you expect those bulls to be here?"

"Probably just a couple of days. I'm riding to the ranch tomorrow and likely there will be someone here the next day to take them off your hands."

"Sure ain't no trouble long as you buy the feed. There's already been four or five ranchers here looking them over. Can't figure out how you could find twelve bulls so alike in age and all."

"Well, I'll tell you sometime maybe but it was someone else's misfortune that caused that many young bulls to be around."

"Anyway, it wouldn't be no problem to sell the lot if they were for sale."

"I guess that's up to Papa now. Here's four bits for the kid for forkin' that hay. I'm going to get some sleep. I want to get started early tomorrow. You sure we're all square now, Charlie?"

"Sure, Jed. Like I say, I got lots of use out of them horses you left here."

Jed had breakfast at the hotel and asked the cook to give him a bag of bread, beef and cheese, enough for the noon meal and some coffee beans. He'd dig his coffee pot out of his gear at the stable. He'd gone without his coffee enough times on this trip.

He headed for the ranch and set a pace that would get him to a spring about the right time for a noon'an.

About the time he was reaching the spring, he saw a rider coming from the ranch. He hoped it wasn't John.

As the rider drew nearer, he recognized Stan Murphy, one of the hands from the ranch. Probably takin' a few days off, he assumed, now that things were slack for the summer. As Stan rode up, he looked at Jed in surprise.

"Jed, I heard you were in Texas. I give up on you ever comin' back."

"I finally found them bulls Papa sent me after. Got them penned behind the livery. Step down, Stan, I'm going to make some coffee and I got a bit of grub. You gather some wood while I get this stuff laid out here and get some water. I'm going to send some boys in after them bulls so you might as well wait around and give them a hand coming back."

"Well, Jed, it ain't likely I'll be back. John's made it plain he's running things now. You know I only stayed around because you and me, we sort of done our own thing although we did all the chores the rest didn't want to do."

"I can't say as I blame you but hang around town anyway till I get back in. Don't be hiring on with anyone. I got a feelin' you'd make a good Texan. What do you think?"

"I'm thinkin' you found something down south to your liking."

"I got an offer to be foreman, that much I know. And the outfit sure could use another man who doesn't mind workin' with his hands. How's Ben? He just letting John run things?"

"Yeh, he spends a lot of time up at Rose's lately. Sure a change for him. I didn't hear John talking against Del anymore either since you boys had that dust up out on the range that day."

"Well, I don't think I persuaded him about anything. Ben must have laid down the law. It's good that Papa and Rose have made up."

"Yes, it surely is. That Del is a good man. I don't know what he's got in mind with that corn and oats he's got planted but I've a feeling he's got a plan and I think your Pa has taken to Del's ideas. I saw him one day setting what looked to me to be a corner cairn on the southeast corner about two miles below Del and Rose's place. What would that be about? Would he be thinking of splitting the *Rocking O*? If he is, he should give the rest to you."

"No, I think I know what he's got in mind. John doesn't know but that old homestead where Del and Rose live, that was where Papa was born. It belonged to my grandmother. When she died, it became Papa's but it's not really part of the *Rocking O* that great grandfather told Papa to leave to John."

"Ain't that something. It looks to me like Ben's going to turn that old place over to Rose and Del."

"From what you're telling me, it sure seems that way. Was Papa home when you rode out?"

"Yes, he was and I expect he still is. I went up to the house to say goodbye before I left. When I told him I just had to leave, he just told me goodbye and maybe I could find something better. Didn't try to talk me out of leaving or nothing."

"Well, I'm going to get this gear back on my horse and head for the ranch. You stay in town now. I won't be more than a couple of days."

"Texas does sound interesting and we always did work well together. I'll see you when you get back in town then."

Jed got the horse loaded again and mounted up. If he hurried, he might have time to talk to his father before John came in from work.

When he got to the ranch, he rode right up to the verandah and left his horse saddled. He didn't want to waste time unsaddling. Anyway, Gimpy was coming up from the stable.

"Jed, you finally got back. I thought you must have been caught in some female's trap. That's the only thing could keep a man away that long."

"Well, I had a piece to go to find twelve bulls but I got us some down in Texas. A place called Breckenridge is the nearest town though it ain't much anymore. Take my horse would you, Gimpy. I want to see Pa before John comes in."

"I reckon your Pa must be sleeping else he would have heard you ride in. Yeh, sure, I'll look after your horse. Good to see you back."

Jed hurried into the house and sure enough his father was stretched out on his bed asleep.

"Papa, wake up. Is this what you been doin' since I went away, sleeping all day?"

"Well, heavens, it's Jed boy. Made it did you? Did you get those bulls I sent you for?"

"I surely did, Papa. Twelve Herefords about fifteen months old. Got them in the livery corral in town. Even got the *Rocking O* brand on them."

"I'm surely glad you made it back alright. I sent you away for more than those bulls. I had to find out what you'd do on your own. You haven't had much chance to be on your own before."

"Papa, it surely did cross my mind that there was more than those bulls you wanted out of that trip. I met Stan on his way into town. Said he was all done."

"Yes, I was sorry to see him go but there's not much can be done about that. I'm going to move up with Rose and Del

71

in the next few days and give this place over to John. As soon as he comes in, I'm going to explain myself to you and John about what I've been doing since you left but let's you and me have a drink and you can tell me about your trip."

For the next twenty minutes, Jed explained about his search for bulls and finally getting them at the Pritchard ranch.

"Kind of lucky for us this Miss Pritchard came along. You say she's getting things straightened out now?"

"When I left, she had five hands branding and gathering for a shipment."

"Anything that might go wrong?"

"Well, she had an overdue mortgage that's been troubling me some."

"So when are you going back down there?"

"I figured if everything came together right, maybe in a couple of days."

"I suppose it takes awhile to go way down there. I saw your horse at the livery in town and asked Charley what he was doing with your horse. He gave me your note and told me you had left on the stage. I never thought of that. I hear the crew coming in. Do you suppose you and John might be civil till after supper then I'm going to tell you both what I've decided. I guess my family won't be together much longer but at least it will be alive and happier than it was before."

Just then John came in.

"I thought that was your horse in the corral. I hadn't seen it around here for so long, I wasn't sure."

"Jed's had a long trip and he did find some young bulls. He left them in the corral behind the livery in town."

"I don't know why we had to have those bulls anyway. He's been gone long enough to go to England for them."

"Have a drink, John and get washed up for supper. After supper, I need to talk to you and Jed. Jed you might want to go and say hello to the boys in the bunkhouse."

"Yes, I guess you're right, Papa. I've been gone so long, they've probably divided up my gear."

The boys were glad to see him but they were sad to hear that he was leaving again. Some of them he knew would be pulling out next payday, if not before. They were good men and they'd get hired on somewhere. He hoped John could replace them before winter. Winter in this north country could mean trouble on a cattle ranch. Not every winter but you could never tell when you'd get a bad one. Oh, well, it wasn't his headache anymore.

He gathered up what few things he had left behind when he headed for Texas, nothing much except some winter clothes. He didn't know if he would need them in Texas or not. He hadn't heard much about the winters there.

They had a quiet supper in the cookhouse where everyone seemed to feel the tension in the air. Then Ben, John and Jed went back to the house and Ben told them to come into the office.

"Sit down, boys and don't look so sober although this could be the last time you see each other.

"John, for the last ten years you've given the impression that the ranch was already yours. Well, from right now, it is. Here's the deed and it's already registered at the land office. I've had a map drawn of all the holdings of the *Rocking O*.

"Now, John, you will notice that some of the land the *Rocking O* uses is not on the deed. All this darkened canyon to the southwest, that's government ground. Your great grandfather was shrewd enough to know if he got his men to homestead the land at the end of those canyons, nobody else would make a claim. To the north, you'll see that the land Del and Rose are living on doesn't belong to the *Rocking O*, either. That belonged to Mother and she left it to me. I've seen fit to deed that section to Rose and Del."

John started to bluster but Ben put his hand up.

"Hold on, John till I'm finished then you can have your say."

"I'm moving up there with Del and Rose. If you don't want Del to ride for you anymore, he may wish to move the *Rocking O* cattle off his property. That's up to you and Del but remember, he has every right.

"As for Jed, he's made it plain to me that he's leaving so you don't need to fight anymore. I have some money in a separate account that Mother left and I'm giving most of that to Jed so he can get set up somewhere of his choosing. Now Jed says he has a dozen good Hereford bulls in the corral behind the livery so if you want them, you'll have to send someone in to bring them here."

"I don't need any of those short legged critters around here. Do whatever you want with them. I couldn't be bothered!"

"Suit yourself. You're the boss here now so let's see what you can do. I guess that's about all I've got to say. If you've anything to say to me, get it off your chest. I'll be moving tomorrow."

"Damn poor time for Jed to pull out! I'm short a man already and roundup's coming in a couple of weeks."

"Don't start that now, John. You lost your best man this morning, whatever you did to get Stan to quit."

"I haven't liked him since he's first been here. He's done nothin' but cozy up to Jed, like Jed owned the place."

"Well, John, for far too long you've used Jed as your slave and whipping boy. He's always taken everything you said to him and never answered back but the day you laid a hand on him, that was all over for him and myself. From now on, you stand on your own feet. There won't be myself or Jed to help you out."

"I don't need you and I don't need Jed and for damn sure I don't need those twelve bulls he spent a month rounding up!"

Jed got to his feet. "If that's all, Papa, I'm going to ride on up to Del's place. I should get there before they go to bed."

"Sure and I forgot to tell you, you're an uncle again. Rose had her baby and it's a boy this time. I've spent the last week and a half helping out up there. Tell Rose I'll be there for lunch tomorrow."

Chapter 7

Jed got his horse out of the corral and saddled up. The horse wasn't in favour of going any further that day but Jed convinced him. This was the only horse he owned and he wasn't about to ride out on one of John's.

An hour and a half later, he could see the lighted window so he knew they were still up. When he rode into the yard, he hailed the house and Del came to the door.

"Who's out there?"

"It's me. Jed."

"Well, come on in! I'll go see to your horse. Rose has been frettin' for weeks about what might have happened to you. Had you killed in a stampede, gored by a bull and drowned in a flood. I never heard of so many ways a man could be killed."

When Jed stepped through the door, Rose flew into his arms.

"Oh, Jed, I'm so glad to see you. Wait till you see the new baby! And little Ruthie, she'll be so happy to see you but she's asleep now. When did you eat last?"

"I had supper at the ranch then Papa filled me in on what's been going on. He gave John the deed to the *Rocking O,* said he was moving up here. What's that all about, Rose?"

"Well, you know, Del's had some ideas about what he could do with this place and Papa, he thought Del might be right so he gave this section to Del and me. Since then, Papa's been up here a lot. He told me you might be leaving so I asked him to move up here. Papa and John, they don't pull too good and anyway Papa has gotten some of his old energy back and he's helpin' Del around here and me, too when I was in bed with the baby."

"Papa said to tell you he'd be here in time for lunch tomorrow. Seems he's bringing his belongings."

"How was your trip, Jed? You must have gone a long ways. Did you get those bulls?"

"Yeah, sure did and good ones, too, half way across Texas but John says he doesn't want them!"

"He'll never change, will he?"

"No, I guess not but I've got an idea about those bulls. Would Del's plans include some cattle?"

"Yes, they surely do."

"Well, let's wait till he comes in before we say any more. You look tired, Rose. Sit down before you fall."

"To tell the truth, I am kind of shaky. I haven't recovered yet from the birthing and I was truly worried about you being gone so long. How long can you stay?"

"Just tomorrow. I've got those bulls to look after and then something tells me I'm needed somewhere."

"I think you've found a woman! Who is it, Jed and where is she?"

"I took on a foreman job down where I bought those bulls and then as soon as I had the bulls ready to travel, I up and left. That just ain't right."

"We'll make the most of tomorrow then. It's hard to say when we'll see each other again. All these changes coming so quick ... I can't keep my head straight."

At that moment, Del came in.

"Sure used that old nag up today, Jed."

"I did but I couldn't change horses at the ranch. Papa gave John the deed to the ranch tonight and that horse is the only thing that truly belongs to me."

"I gave him some corn and hay and left him a bucket of water. He'll be fine when you need him again."

"Rose tells me you plan to have some cattle on this place sometime soon."

"I sure would like to have a few but I can't afford any right now."

"I think I've got an idea how you might get some but we'll wait till Papa gets here tomorrow. It's sure good that you and Papa have finally gotten together."

"Well, Jed, he's just as sweet now as he's been sour for the last two years."

"He's been regretting for a long time about not seeing Rose and his granddaughter. It took that little dust up John and I had to make him realize he was losing out on his family. Finally, he asked if Rose would make him welcome and I told him Rose would love to have him visit. I didn't know what you'd think but I figured if Rose was glad to see Papa, you wouldn't say anything."

"It sure did surprise me when I rode in one day and he was here. In an hour's time, everything was dandy. He asked me what I'd do with this place if it was mine and I told him. Ten days later, he brings the deed, says the place is ours."

"He told John and me tonight that he had some money grandmother left that he was giving to me. Didn't say how much. Is he going to be alright here?"

"Oh, sure. Papa won't give you his last cent. He plans to get Del some machine he ordered in town. It's coming from Illinois. It's supposed to shell corn somehow. Del near wore himself out last fall shelling that corn by hand."

"Well, I have my bedroll with me so I'll just bed down in the barn. Mind if I take this lantern along?"

"Go ahead. It'll be daylight by the time I'm ready to feed the stock."

"Good night. Get some rest, Rose."

"I'll try but the baby gets me up a couple of times in the night. Del can't feed him what he needs so that's my job."

Jed went out to the barn and found his gear where Del had put it then found some hay and laid his bedroll down. For over a week now, he'd slept in the hay. He was getting used to it. He fell asleep thinking how Ben had planned everything out.

In the morning, he was up and dressed before Del came out from the house. He fed his horse and Del's while Del fed the hens and pigs.

"You've made a pretty good start here, Del. Must have taken some lookin' to find hens around here."

"Got them in town. Traded corn for six hens and a rooster last year. Raised six more chickens into hens and cooked up what roosters were in the brood. That pig, he'll eat most anything, loves the weeds from the garden and any kitchen scraps we have. I'm thinking that next year I might plant some potatoes and see if we have a long enough season or enough rain."

"You keep this up and you won't have time for a paying job. That reminds me, Papa told John that if he didn't want you riding for him no more, you would probably want him to move his cattle off this place."

"As long as John doesn't cause trouble, he can use this range till I get money to stock it. It's got the best winter feed of any of the range. Might be a bit inconvenient for anyone from the ranch in winter, if the snow's deep. For me, it's easy. I'm in the middle of the section, more or less and it's not much more than a mile to the farthest areas where the cattle stay in winter."

"Well, don't expect John to realize the benefits of having you look out for his interests. He's so contrary, if he had rabies, he'd bite himself."

"Let's get washed up. Rose will be hollerin' any minute."

As they came to the door, Jed could smell bacon frying and fresh biscuits. The aroma from the coffee was so powerful, his taste buds were making him drool.

Young Ruthie came running when she saw him and he picked her up.

"Uncle Jed, you came back."

"Oh, sure. I forgot to say goodbye to you."

"Well, don't say goodbye, ever."

"Ever is a long time and you'll have Papa here with you now."

"Yeah, Papa likes me."

"I like you, too but let's get us some of those biscuits before your Daddy takes them all."

"Mama says she cooked special just for you."

"Here, let me take her, Jed. I need to feed her slow so she doesn't choke on anything."

Just as they finished breakfast, the baby started to fuss and Rose brought him out for Jed to see. Likely he was wet so Jed didn't want to hold him. He had held other newborn things before but this was different. To think he might drop such a squirmy thing or hold it wrong. It looked so helpless! He supposed Rose would have him cleaned up and ready at lunchtime and he'd have to hold it but he'd make sure he was sitting down.

Del proclaimed that he was taking the morning off. He took Jed back outside and showed him around and told him all his ideas and some of Ben's.

"Your father has lots of ideas and they're good ones but he doesn't realize that they take money. I have to restrict myself to ideas that only need labour."

As they progressed along, Jed could see that Del couldn't restrain himself from work. He'd check a corral post or check the roofs of the buildings for lifted shingles. Everywhere they walked, they were faced with something to do. Finally, Jed asked him what he would be doing if he wasn't around.

"Well, I've got that acre of corn to harvest. Most of the ears are ripe and ready."

"Let's get to it. I'll lend you a hand."

"Rose would hang me. This is your last day around these parts."

"We'll just work till lunch. Papa will be here then."

So they set to work with Del showing Jed what to look for and which ears might not be ripe.

"I'll come back in about a week and pick the rest. There might be some that we miss today that will be past their prime but it will make pig feed if it's boiled a bit. The pigs will eat cob and all. Soon as we get caught up, Ben and me, we're going to make a smoker, get more pigs and sell bacon and hams. Reckon I'll need some transportation between here and town."

"Sounds like you're going to be quite the business man ... corn, oats, now hams and sides of bacon."

"And beef, too if I can get my hands on enough money to get started. I figure I can take a beef to town every trip and sell it to the butcher. Most times, he has to go out and buy from a rancher and bring the critter in himself. I could deliver one every time I go to town or even two tied behind the wagon."

"I think, Del, you're going to do alright here."

"What about you, Jed? Seems to me you came out short when Ben divided up his belongings."

"I think it's as fair as he could do. He couldn't divide the *Rocking O*. That would defeat his whole purpose and he certainly couldn't divide the one section he gave to you and Rose. He said he had some money for me that grandmother left him. I don't feel right taking it. I'm going to send a letter back to you saying where I am and if Papa ever needs money, you or Rose write me and I'll see that he gets taken care of."

"Jed, as long as this place can make us a living, your Pa

81

will be alright here with us. We're going to build a small cabin this fall for your Pa. Course he'll take his meals with us but he'll have a place to hide when the kids get too much for him. Well, look how much we've done. Time sure does go faster if you have someone to talk to. Been ridin' alone up in this end for two years now. Gettin' into the habit of talking to myself and me less than thirty years old. Let's go sit on the porch till Ben comes. I'm anxious to hear what you have to say that's so secret."

"It ain't a secret. It's just that it needs Papa's approval and I didn't want to make false promises."

About eleven o'clock, Ben drove in with a buckboard loaded up with his stuff. Jed and Del took the horse and buckboard to the barn while Ben sat with little Ruthie on the porch.

"Papa, Uncle Jed come'd last night while I was sleeping. Mama says Uncle Jed has to go away again. Is that why you look sad, Papa?"

"Well, I reckon it is, Ruthie but you and me we shouldn't be thinking just about what we want. You see, Jed is a grown up man. He needs to go away where he can find his own place and meet a woman and get married so he can have kids of his own, little ones like you and your new brother."

"Mama says the baby hasn't got a name yet and she wants to name it before Uncle Jed goes away."

"Maybe we can do that this afternoon then we'll celebrate. How would that be?"

"What's celibate?"

"That's when you're happy about something and you share your happiness with friends and family."

"I like that, Papa, we celibate."

When Del and Jed came in from the barn, Ruthie jumped down and ran inside. They could hear her talking to her mother.

"Mama, Papa says we name the baby and celibate. You want to celibate, Mama? Papa says Uncle Jed's going to get married and have kids just like me."

"You telling the youn'un winders, Papa?"

"Just sayin' what's on my mind. You probably already found a woman when you were in Texas. You're in an all fired hurry to get back there."

"Let's leave that be for now, Papa. I have an idea about those bulls in town but I need your approval."

"I don't care to claim them, either. You spent a month finding them and John doesn't want them. I take it he hasn't paid you for the time you were away so I say they're yours. If you have an idea let's hear it."

"Del says he'd like to start raising a few head of cattle and he sure could use a couple of those bulls here. Charlie at the livery thinks maybe he should keep a bull out back and charge a fee for it's use. It seems no one in town has a bull for all the milk cows in the area. That still leaves nine and Charlie tells me there's been a lot of ranchers looking them over.

"What if I gave Del those bulls to trade for breeding stock? Most likely the cows would already be with calf but that would give him a start all that much sooner. I spent about a hundred and thirty dollars for each bull, counting my travelling and shipping plus sixty for each bull. I expect you could maybe swap them, three or four to one for cows to anyone who knows what he's about. These Herefords are far better in my book."

"You going to be around to make this swap?"

"No, I can't stay but you come on into town with me tomorrow and we'll get things started."

"What do you think, Del? We're kind of talking over your head."

"Sure would give me a jump start here but like Jed says,

those bulls are worth a hundred and thirty dollars apiece and I couldn't buy one horn."

"Well, they're no good to me and there's plenty more on that ranch in Texas. I've got to get them out of that corral before I go. I'll make you and Rose a present of two bulls for a wedding gift. It seems I never got around to giving you one. It was Papa's money I spent to get the bulls so I leave Papa to do what he wants with the nine not spoken for."

"Del and I will think about that. There sure is a need for money around here to get everything done that Del has in mind."

"I like the idea of getting some cows. Maybe first time heifers with calf. We could have calves here early next spring then breed them to those Herefords. That's about as fast as we can get the cattle end of things started. What about Charlie, would he pay a hundred and thirty dollars for one of those bulls?"

"All we can do is ask. We'll owe him something for looking after them anyways and he might help you with the sales. We could maybe give him a discount. If we do it this way, I can get on my way to Texas day after tomorrow. By the way, Papa, I'm taking Stan with me. He and I work well together and I might feel more at home there if I have someone from here with me."

"What's your all fired rush, Jed?"

"I don't know. I got that ranch out of a sorry mess but I have a feeling I took it from the frying pan into the fire. The ranch is owned by a woman. Her Pa died over a year before. There was a horse rancher in the area hanging around harassing her and he had her cowhands beaten up and run off till she had no crew left.

"I started a crew rounding up a herd for market but there's also a mortgage long past due. What would happen if the bank decided to foreclose. There's eight thousand acres of deeded land and all the stock that's been left to accumulate for the past year and half. The bank could demand all payment of that mortgage any time, couldn't it, Papa?"

"Yes, you're probably right but surely they would let her sell the herd and catch up the back payments."

"Well, according to what Rolly told me, he's the guy who stays around the place something like old Gimpy here, he says they've never heard from that banker in all this time. I'm thinking there's a reason for that ... a bank waiting till they get so far behind that they won't have any trouble getting foreclosure papers signed with short notice!"

"Well, by dang, Jed, you've been listening to what's been going on around here while you've been slaving away for John and me. I expect the same thing to happen to the *Rocking O* but it's out of my hands. Okay then, I see your point so I'll go to town tomorrow and take the buckboard. When I come back, I might as well bring back those two bulls."

Just then Rose called them all to lunch.

"I'm afraid I've got just about the same as we had for breakfast ... biscuits, bacon and eggs. It has to be something fast these days and we have our own bacon and eggs so it doesn't cost so much."

"Rose, you're doing fine and wait till you hear what Jed and Ben have come up with."

"I guess I heard most of it and I'm grateful to you, Papa and you, Jed."

"Well, Rose, I can't be waiting around to sell those bulls and it's Papa's money I spent to get them. It seems he's got a reason for you and Del to get things going here as fast as you can."

"That wasn't the most interesting thing I heard you talkin' of out there. I heard that ranch down in Texas was owned by a woman. Now, how old would this woman be, Jed?"

"I don't exactly know, Rose. I didn't ask to see her teeth. I wasn't there but a week."

"You were there plenty of time to make you want to rush back."

"Well, you see, Rose I'm thinkin' there might be a banker just waitin' to get his hands on that ranch. It's a nice spread worth three or four times what Rolly told me the mortgage was for. I'm only wanting to do what I can for Miss Ellen."

"Oh, my, she even has a title. You hear that, Del. Miss Ellen, he says!"

"That's what everyone calls her, even other women. Seems she has everyone's respect around there. It's just proper that I call her what everyone else does."

"Speaking of callin' someone by a name, Ruthie says we're going to name the baby this afternoon and then 'celibate', as she says."

"That we are, Rose. It ain't right for Jed to ride away down to Texas without knowing what we're going to call his first nephew."

"Del and I can't agree with anything we've come up with. We tried not to get our hopes up that it would be a boy this time so we didn't try to find a name. What do you think, Papa? Any family names you want to mention?"

"No, we've already got a Jed, and John was named after Holly's father, John Benson and my father Johnny Owens. Lord knows, we don't want two Bens around here. What about you, Jed, you got an idea?"

"How about Stan? As I've told Papa, I'm taking Stan Murphy to Texas with me. I think he'd be proud if you used his name. You and Stan got along good, didn't you, Del?"

"We surely did. That would be alright with me, Rose, if you like the idea."

"What do you think, Papa?"

"Sounds fine with me. How about you, Ruthie, can the baby be called Stan?"

"Fine by me, Papa. Now we going to 'celibate'?"

"I might have a few swallows of whiskey left in a bottle in

TEXAS BOUND   Arnold McKay

that stuff you boys unloaded in the back. I'll go get it. What
about you, Rose. You going to toast the new baby's name?"

"Ruthie and I will find something to drink. You boys go
ahead while I check my cupboards."

When Rose checked, she found peppermint in a small
container and she made herself and Ruthie a drink of
peppermint, generously sweetened. After the men got a bit of
whiskey in their cups, they all toasted the new baby, Stan.

When Ruthie tasted her drink, she looked at her mother
and said, "I like to celibate."

Everybody laughed and then Ben got serious.

"To think it took a near disaster to bring this happy
occasion about. Jed makes light of the trouble between
himself and John but I got the story from the boys that John
would have shot Jed that day. Then where would I be right
now. I expect John will lose the *Rocking O*. He can't keep
good men. They won't work for him. Jed and me, we always
was sort of a buffer between John and the men. He's already
lost two of the best, with Stan Murphy the most recent and if
he tells Del he can't work for him anymore, he'll be mighty
short handed for round up."

"Well, if you men will take your 'celibation' somewhere
else, I'll get some work done here so we can have a rest
before I need to get supper."

The men filed out and headed for the barn to get Ben fixed
up as comfortable as possible. When they got there, Ben
pulled another bottle from his bedroll.

"You boys bring your cups. I didn't pull this one, didn't
want Rose to think we was all going to get drunk, as Ruthie
says, 'celibatin'. Now Jed, I want to hear a little more about
this trip of yours and about that ranch down there in Texas. I
see you favouring that right hand some. Is there a story
behind that?"

"Well, there's a lesson anyways, Papa. Don't hit a bonehead
with your fist. Get a club or something."

"I take it that wasn't the end of it. You wouldn't be back here if he was still a threat."

"When he came to his feet, he challenged me with guns the next day in Richardson in front of the livery and I thought that if he was paying for the tune, we should dance. After he rode away, my hand started swelling up and everybody was saying how I'd have to duck out. I didn't have a left hand holster with me but I managed to get an old saddle maker in Breckenridge to make me one. When he found out what I needed it for, he made me a first class holster. Didn't want to take anything for it.

"I let it be known I had a bad right hand. I was afraid Artie Smith, that was the man, he might back out or have the Marshall call the whole thing off. I needed to get rid of him before I left there, you see."

"Did you kill him, Jed?"

"No, I only wounded him but he'll have a stiff right arm the rest of his life and I expect by the time he's recovered, he won't have much left to stay around for. He wasn't very well liked."

"When you go back down there, Jed, you be careful. If what you fear is fact, you'll be a threat to some person or people who could have you taken care of."

"Give me that bottle, Papa. This 'celebatin' is gettin' too serious. Now let's hear what you and Del have been hatchin' up for this old homestead."

"Well, this fall we got our hands full. Got an acre of corn to gather, an acre of oats, and a cabin to build for me before it gets too cold to sleep here in the barn and Del wants to get a smoke house built.

"We will need to hunt winter meat but I reckon the hunting won't be too hard with that acre of oats there. I expect as soon as the weather cools a bit, we'll have our hands full to keep the elk out of the field till the oats get ripe enough to thrash by hand. We got a machine ordered that is supposed to shell corn. Maybe that will be in when we get to town tomorrow."

"Jed and I harvested almost half of that corn this morning just walkin' the rows and talking and picking. First thing you know, we're half done."

"That's good, Del because I can see that I'll be gone at least three days, maybe four going to Cheyenne. If I bring them bulls back, I'll need to take the second day for sure coming back. You want I should get us some help for a week or so?"

"How would I pay them, Ben?"

"Don't worry about that. I'm more worried about the work we need to do. We can't have the harvest get ruined."

"Well, all I've got to donate to this project is muscle. You do what you think needs doing."

"We surely can't stand any set backs or lost time. Now, let's have another go at that bottle. There's just about enough for a drink apiece."

They went up to the cabin and spent the rest of the evening just chatting away, trying to forget that Jed was leaving the next morning and finally Ben said he was tired and needed to get his sleep if he was to go to Cheyenne the next day.

Rose asked Del if he would stay inside and keep an ear open for the children. She wanted Jed to walk with her a ways.

As soon as they were clear of the house, she spoke what was on her mind.

"Jed, I want you to know you've been the best possible brother that a girl could hope for. You've always been good to me and the way you looked after Mother when she was ill and dying, well, I just want to say that if you find the right girl, don't sell yourself short even if she owns a big ranch. If she likes you, there's no reason to feel you're not bringing enough to the table. Any woman who sees in you what I see will be glad to get you, flat broke or otherwise. If you get married, I want you to promise me you'll bring your wife for a visit as soon as you can. It's not just for me but Papa needs to see you happy. I guess you can see that."

"I guess you're right, Rose. Papa hasn't been himself since Mama died and now he's kind of taking a hold of life again so anything that keeps him going the way Del has him going now, I'm all for that."

"He sent you after those bulls you know just to see how you would handle yourself. When he came back from that week in Cheyenne he was all smiles, said Jed's a lot smarter than me. He's left everything at the livery and went south on the stage. But he was getting worried. You were gone so long.

Well, I guess we should get back. We're going to miss you, Jed but I know it's for the best. If you're ever busted and need a place to hang out, remember where we live and write us sometimes."

"I'm glad we had this talk, Rose. I expect Papa will be on that wagon bright and early and we won't have much time in the morning."

Chapter 8

Down in Richardson, Amos Mason was celebrating with a drink. He seldom drank and just as rarely came into a saloon but today had been fruitful. He had finally cornered the Sheriff and had him take the foreclosure notice out to the Pritchard place that afternoon. He sure hadn't made friends with the Judge or the Sheriff, especially when the Sheriff found out that the owner was waiting for a cattle buyer.

The Sheriff had reported back that he served the paper and then he had given Mason a grilling. Why didn't he let the woman sell her stock and make a payment on the mortgage? Amos stuck to his guns saying the payments were in default and he had every right to foreclose on every animal on the place. Word must be getting around because people were giving him some pretty strange looks.

Then he heard one man saying, "I wouldn't want to be in his shoes when that Owens fellow gets back to town. He took that Artie Smith out left handed, let Artie start his draw first so they tell me. Knocked Artie ass over teakettle the day before and broke his right hand. Got old man Estey to work all night to make that left hand holster. Old man Estey is still showing up for drinks and ready to tell us all about it."

Amos got up and walked out. Now, how was he getting out of this. He had no idea that Owens would ever be back. The talk was now that there was a spark between the Miss Pritchard and Owens. All he could hope was that Owens would not show up until after the date of foreclosure. Ten days. They certainly would be long ones.

Meanwhile, out at the Pritchard ranch, things were pretty gloomy. Everyone crowded around the table, all talking at once.

"Miss Ellen, I've got to send a telegram to Jed."

"No, Ricky. If you do, you'll be saying I expect him to come up with eleven thousand dollars. That's the only way we can fix this problem."

"What I don't understand is why the bank won't let you ship that beef. You could pay some on the mortgage."

"That's not what they want here, Chad. It's the ranch. Don't you think so, Miss Ellen?"

"I'm afraid you're right, Rolly. They never bothered about the missed payments, just let them stack up to where any Judge would have to agree to sign that foreclosure. I'm afraid, boys we're stopped in our tracks. Ten days from now, we won't have a ranch."

"I still say we should send a telegram. If Owens can't help, at least give him the chance to try or even if what Miss Ellen says, that he has no obligation, let him know what the situation is. Maybe, if he can't help, he'll just stay home. After all, he was willing to leave one ranch up in Wyoming for a foreman job here. Maybe if he knew we don't have a ranch any longer, he'll want to stay where he is."

"I suppose you're right, Ricky. There's no point of him coming back down here if he has a good position where he is."

"Excuse me for saying, Miss Ellen but I kind of figured his interest wasn't just in the ranch."

"How could it be anything else. He was only here a few days."

"Strange man that Mr. Owens. Seems to size up things mighty quick. Ever notice, Miss Ellen, most men treat you with great respect and all but they don't try to cozy up to you. I reckon it's your height. Rather intimidating for most men but not for Mr. Owens now. You kind of have to look up to him, Miss Ellen, in more ways than one."

As Rolly finished his speech, Miss Ellen's cheeks were fiery red.

"See now what I mean, boys. She's blushin'. I knew that day when he went to meet Artie Smith, the way she pined away. Now I figure that if this Owens is the man I think he is and knowing that you're strapped for cash down here, he's going to come with whatever he's got coming up there in Wyoming. You got to figure a few things.

"First, he's trustworthy enough that his father sent him down here with money enough to buy those bulls and with judgement enough to get what was needed.

"Second thing you got to look at is, if that ranch up there is that kind of going concern to be sending him way down here, there's got to be money.

"Third thing is, why was he so quick to say he'd come back here to be foreman? It could be that he's already been cut free from his moorings up there. If he's got money, he could help you, Miss Ellen. Whether he's got romantic interests or not, you could make a deal. Take him on as a partner. I'm all for sending the telegram but not just to head him off. That will be his decision but to let him know the straight of it and offer a partnership. What do you say, Miss Ellen?"

"Rolly, I haven't known you to make so much sense in a coon's age. Most times you make a speech, you could put it in one sentence. What do you think, Ricky? You rode with him more than the rest of us. Did he seem interested in the place?"

"Never asked many questions but he looked the place over sharp. I think Rolly put the thing mighty straight. Now we got to get the telegram writ out and say a lot in a few words and then hope he hasn't left Cheyenne yet. The only thing we know is he lives a bit northwest of Cheyenne and he did tell me to send a telegram to Cheyenne if we had more problems than we could handle. You write up what you want to say, Miss Ellen and I'll get it to town. The station stays open all night."

"What can I possibly say in a telegram that doesn't sound like a helpless female begging for a man?"

"I'll tell you what to say if you do the writing, Miss Ellen. I ain't too good at that. I'll sign the telegram. How would that be?"

"Lord help me, I don't know what I'd do without you boys. I gave up as soon as the Sheriff left here this afternoon. Okay, what do you want me to write?"

"Mortgage foreclosure ten days. Stop. Eleven thousand dollars. Stop. Miss Ellen would consider partnership. Stop."

"Ricky, you got everything in just a few words. It doesn't hardly seem possible."

"I been composin' that thing ever since this afternoon and I'd have sent it anyway whether we convinced you or not. I just needed you to say you'd take on a partner. Now I'm getting this on the wire tonight. If we haven't already missed him, we probably won't. Most likely he'd check the telegraph office before he boards the train."

When Ricky reached town, he got the same agent Jed had talked to about shipping bulls and who had peddled the information to Artie Smith.

As soon as the message was sent, the agent headed for Amos Mason's house. That kind of information should be worth more than a drink or two. There was talk around town that Amos Mason was somehow going to foreclose on the Pritchard ranch. That telegram was from the Pritchard place although it was signed by Ricky and it was sent to that jasper

94

from Wyoming.

He had to be careful what he said to Mason and not give too much away until he got his money. When he arrived at Mason's house, the light was still on so he knocked. Mason answered right away.

"You're Wally from down at the station, aren't you?   Do you have a message for me?"

"I got a message you might want to know about and for the right price, I might let you see it."

"How do I know what the right price is, if I don't see it."

"Let's just say, it's from the Pritchard gal to Cheyenne."

"It might be worth something, I suppose. The bank needs to keep up on what people do who have money loaned to them."

"I ain't breakin' all the rules of the railroad and risking my job for no free drink, I can tell you that."

"How about twenty dollars then but it better be good."

"Oh, I think you might find it interestin' enough to pay say thirty, in advance mind you."

"All right. Wait here till I get the money and this better be worth it."

When Wally had the money in his hand, he passed Amos a copy of the telegram.

"Nice doin' business with you, Mr. Mason."

"If there's anything more, Wally, bring it to me. I'll pay the same price."

After the station agent left, Mason paced the floor and tried to see what this meant. Would Owens come down here from Wyoming with enough money to free up that mortgage? It wasn't likely. He heard that he had accepted a job at the Pritchard ranch as foreman so he was sure that he didn't own a ranch in Wyoming. There was no way he could see him having eleven thousand dollars.

Then again, if he had someone to back him, he could

borrow that amount. If he did, he would probably have it on him when he arrived. Without money, Owens would be helpless. The thing to do was make sure he didn't keep the money long enough after he arrived to get here to the bank.

But he probably wouldn't come straight to the bank. He would have to see the Pritchard woman first and make some sort of a deal.

Somehow, he had to find a man or two to relieve Owens of his money before he had a chance to do anything. There was nothing to be done at the moment. If Owens got the telegram right away, it would take four or five days for him to arrive and he might send word of his arrival time, if he was coming at all. Wally, down at the station would let him know and then he could arrange a reception committee somehow.

He didn't know anyone he could hire but he could find someone. If Owens was carrying enough money for the mortgage, there were lots of men who would be glad of the chance to relieve him of the money. Some of those men who worked for Artie Smith might want a chance to even the score.

Tomorrow, first thing, he would ride out to Artie's place and see what he could do with some of those men. He knew Artie was still at the doctors house and might be there for some time.

Things seemed to be happening that he hadn't thought of but he would just have to let things play out now that he had started the ball rolling. Maybe he would run out of string. There was no way of knowing but a man couldn't make much working in a bank handling money for someone else.

It was morning at Del and Rose's place and Jed and Ben were hitching up the buckboard. Rose came out of the house with Ruthie hanging to her dress tail and the baby in her arms.

"Okay, Jed, he's all nice and clean so you hold him while

Papa and Del get everything ready. You never can tell, it might not be long before you have one of your own."

Jed was nervous but he didn't want to disappoint Rose so he held out his arms and accepted the little bundle. The morning was cool and the baby was all draped up but suddenly out came two little hands pushing the blanket aside and two little eyes staring him in the face. It sure felt like magic. The little guy could really look you in the eye.

"He certainly is a marvel, Rose. I ain't never seen anything like it."

"Del says the same, that it's all a man needs to keep him busy and his mind from sin."

"I'm going to give him back to you, Rose and pick Ruthie up for a minute or two. I see Papa has the team about ready. No point in me takin' my horse into town. I've decided Stan and me, we're going to go first class on the railroad. I'm sure you and Del can use another horse around here."

"We surely can. That's one thing we are short of, among the many. Next spring, Del wants to get a work team or hire one to do our heavy work. He used an old mule last spring and I swear he pushed that plough more than that old mule pulled."

"Ruthie, are you going to help your Ma with the baby while I'm gone?"

"Yeah, I rock the cradle when he cries."

"That's my girl. I promised your Mother and now I'm going to promise you, I'll come back to visit as soon as I can but I don't know when that will be. You be good and help your Ma. Give me a good hard hug, now."

Jed gave Rose a hug, shook hands with Del and then boosted himself up to the seat of the buckboard. Ben slapped the reins and got the horses moving. It would be a long, full day to Cheyenne.

"I'm glad we're getting this chance together, Jed since

you'll be going away for hard to say how long. First off, I want to tell you why there's money left to me from my Mother. I guess I should start from the first.

"My mother and father settled that place Del and Rose have. When my Father died in an accident, grandfather for reasons only he and mother could understand decided he should take over the mortgage and that mother leave me with him.

"Later, mother married a man by the name of Ed Stouton. They bought a ranch near a town called Trails End up north of here. Ed Stouton was working with a man in town who called himself Al Brighton. They were giving tours of the hot springs west of the Stouton Place. Al Brighton got wind that they were going to make that area a National Park and he talked Ed into a partnership deal.

"Before they could get the papers signed, Ed got a hint about the park and right away Brighton hired a local gun hand to goad Ed into a gunfight where Ed was killed. Then this Brighton, he hired men to terrorize Mother so she would sell and he could buy her out cheap.

"Finally, she sent for me, sayin' she needed help. I wouldn't have gone except grandfather made me promise to at least go and see her. I guess I was getting pretty wild about then. It always ate at me you see that my mother had gone off and left me.

"Anyway, the same day I arrived there, two men rode in. One was the very person who had shot Ed Stouton.

"I was half crazy that my mother would use me this way and I guess I had no fear of dying. I had practised with a gun so I called him out but for some reason, he wouldn't draw. His foreman took up the challenge and I shot him dead.

"Things kind of heated up after that. I sort of forgave Mother once I found out she had been keeping tabs on me over the years and it had been from grandfather's urging that she stay away from me that kept us apart.

"I stayed there till the following spring. In the meantime, I acted as Deputy Sheriff and helped corral Al Brighton and a banker by the name of Hamp Winslow ... not their real names, we found out. I met your mother up there and we were married that spring before we came back south.

"My mother sold the ranch to some syndicate from back east for twenty five thousand dollars. It was the ideal place for those tours that were going to multiply once they approved Yellowstone National Park. The Sheriff that I worked with up there got the job of overseer after he married up with the school teacher, a lady by the name of Grace Hinton. She did wonderful charcoal drawings and she was the means for the Sheriff to capture Al Brighton and the banker, Winslow. Both of them were wanted for murder back east.

"Grace also made pictures of your mother and me and your grandmother and the ranch she had up north. Your grandmother shot a man that winter, too though we told her that it wasn't her bullet that killed him. Mother shot him low down and his partner finished him off to get rid of him but he would have died anyway.

"I've got those pictures with me and I want you to take them. If you're going to start a future, you need to have a past. They're only charcoal and they need care or they'll just fade away or if they get wet, they'll smear so there's no detail left."

"Wouldn't they be safer back at Del and Rose's place, Papa?"

"I suppose they would but Rose is living more or less where she always lived and someday I'll tell her most of what I've told you. You need something from your past to take with you into the future and I think you should take these things and whatever money I can let you have."

"Papa, you should keep the money. You and Del, you could get that place up and running in no time."

"That's a fact, Jed but what satisfaction would Del have in that. I'll buy him a few things to work with to make things go faster, like this corn shredder I'm getting. And those bulls you gave Rose for a wedding present. That's going to be help enough. Let Del do the rest."

"Yes, I guess you're right, Papa. They are giving you a home now so Del and Rose will feel better if you help them a bit but not too much. I can see why Del says all he's got is the muscle."

"Jed, that man's got more ideas for makin' money than you'd believe. Some things don't amount to much but they don't take much work or time, either. Like selling one or two steers at a time to the butcher in town. He has to come every so often anyway for supplies, he might as well tie a couple of steers on the back and make the trip pay. He's always thinking. Rose couldn't have found a better husband and father for her kids."

"It sure makes my leavin' easier, Papa, knowin' you're going to be alright."

"About as right as I can be, knowing that John will probably lose the *Rocking O*. You know and I know he can't keep the good workers. They won't take his abuse, verbal or otherwise. He's already lost two of his regular hands and I expect he'll go over and fire Del by the time I get back.

"These last two winters, Del looked after the stock in that area and before that we kept a man stationed at the old homestead cabin. You've had a few turns there yourself. If John were thinking right, he'd cut his herd at shipping time this fall and if he wants to fire Del, pull all the cattle back closer to the *Rocking O*. It's only a matter of time till Del will put his own cattle in that area anyway. Maybe even some this fall.

"Next spring or fall, we'll probably fence between Del's place and the *Rocking O*. That will make it easier for Del. He can see every cow on the place from top of the barn. Jed, I know and you know there's nothing we can do for John. He has to go his own contrary way. If there was a way I could insure he wouldn't fail, I'd do it. He's my son and that can't be changed.

"Well, that's enough about the problems you're leaving behind. What do you expect will be waitin' down in Texas?"

"Papa, I keep thinkin' about that mortgage and how the bank let it run so long. As I told you, Artie Smith was looking to get hold of that ranch. When I left down there, he was no longer a threat. What if the bank was just waitin' for something like this. If they had foreclosed before, Smith would have put a bid in and seen that everything was done right. Now there's nobody to step in and bid against the bank or someone at the bank. If somebody at the bank has an interest, it's because they want the place themselves. I told Ricky, the guy I left in charge, if there was a problem, to send me a telegram. I should know tomorrow morning."

When they got to Cheyenne, Jed drove the team right up to the livery and unhitched while Ben went off to the hotel.

Charlie came out and greeted him.

"You come for them bulls, Jed?"

"No, I didn't. Papa's going to take a couple back with him though. You want one, Charlie?"

"Don't know as I could afford somethin' like that. How much you asking?

"Well, it seems they cost about a hundred and thirty dollars apiece, Charlie. You know anybody around here who could buy them ten bulls?"

"Maybe not any one man but there's sure been a lot of interest. Been plenty of company around here the last two days."

"From the talk you heard, do you suppose those ranchers would trade some young breedin' heifers, say three or four for one bull?"

"I couldn't say for sure, Jed but we could soon find out and I'll take one myself for a hundred and thirty dollars. I thought you'd be askin' more, seeing as how you were gone for a month. How come you're sellin' them now that you got them here?"

"Well, Papa decided to give the runnin' of the *Rocking O* over to John and he says he's not interested in these here bulls and I've got a job down in Texas."

"Guess you boys could never see eye to eye."

"I'd like to get rid of these critters before the east bound leaves tomorrow. Could you spread the word that I'll be here early to take offers and make the deals?"

"Sure, Jed. I had Stan Murphy in earlier askin' if you had come in. Sold me his horse, he did. He goin' down south with you?"

"Yeah, he sure is. Stan and I get along good together and I sure could use a friend down there that I can depend on. I'll see you in the morning, Charlie. I got to meet Papa at the restaurant before it closes."

As Jed was leaving the stable, he met Stan Murphy coming in.

"Saw Ben headin' into the hotel. Figured likely you were looking after the team."

"Yeah, Papa went ahead to book us rooms then I'm meeting him at Mae's Diner across the street. Have you eaten yet?"

"Yeah, an hour ago but I could have dessert and coffee. Come on, let's get in there before they close and hold a table. I'm kind of excited about this trip but I'll tell you, you'll have to pay my way. I never waited for what John owed me. It wasn't but for a few days anyhow."

"I'll pay you out of the money we get for those bulls tomorrow. They rightfully should have been John's but contrary as he is, he wouldn't accept them because I had picked them out."

"What about your Pa? He sent you after them."

"Papa signed the ranch over to John and he's moved over with Rose and Del. He gave them the section that was the old homestead."

"So that's what he was doing out there that day, fixin' up that boundary cairn. Getting everything exact so there'd be no fighting later."

Just then Ben came into the diner and joined them.

"Hello, Stan. Heard you signed on with an Owens again and you're heading for Texas."

"It will be new country to me, Ben and Jed will be pretty good company."

"Glad you'll be with him. You boys ordered yet?"

"No, we were waiting for you. Mae, what have you got that won't be too much bother to you this late at night?"

"I don't know, the soups getting kind of watery but I could give you a good steak and fried potatoes and I've got some green beans if you don't mind them warmed over."

"That sounds okay and coffee all around. Just pie for Stan. He says he chowed down earlier."

Everyone settled in and finished their meal and soon were on their way to the hotel. Stan turned aside toward the livery.

"Reckon I'll bed down with Charlie at the stable."

"There's no need, Stan. You can sleep in my room."

"No, I told Charlie I'd be back and my bedroll's there. Sold my horse to Charlie today and paid a few bills I had around town. Don't need that horse any more."

"We'll get you mounted on something down there in Texas but it might be a Hereford bull. More cattle than horses on that ranch we're going to. Good night, Stan."

"I'll see you early, Jed."

When they reached the hotel, Ben asked Jed what he found out about the bulls at the livery.

"Charlie says there's been lots of interest and he wants to keep one for himself, like I figured he might. I kind of let it be known we'd trade for some heifers, three for one. That sound alright?"

"I don't think we can do better without hanging around town for a few days. You want to get to Texas and I need to get back to Del's. We've got too much to do before winter. Let's get on up to bed and let tomorrow take care of itself. We've had a long day."

The next morning after breakfast at Mae's Diner, they walked to the livery stable. People had already gathered by the corral and Jed could see that there was plenty of interest.

"Papa, you point out the two you want and Stan and I will rope them out. Then we'll give Charlie a chance to pick out the one he wants."

Twenty minutes later, they were down to nine bulls and pretty near as many interested men waiting to hear the deal.

"Anybody here who wants all nine bulls? We're in a hurry here."

No hands went up.

"What if we split them up in lots of three? Anybody want three? You can have them for cash or we'll take heifers that are bred and will drop a calf between now and next spring. Three heifers for one bull or one hundred and thirty dollars cash. What about you, Mr Jenson? You'd be nice and handy for Ben to pick up them heifers if you was of a mind to trade."

"Yeah, I guess I should try something new now and again. I'll go for three."

"Anybody else got their mind made up?"

Nobody spoke up so Jed told Mr. Jenson to rope out his choice.

"Well, Papa, I guess we'll have to wait for more interest. At least you got Del nine heifers close to home."

"It's early, Jed. I'm sure we can turn the rest to cash or heifers before your train leaves. I checked at the hotel last

104

night. Your train doesn't leave until three thirty and that is if it's on time."

"I'm going down to the station, Papa and get tickets for Stan and myself and see if there's any telegrams from Texas."

As he entered the station, the agent looked up and recognized him.

"Mr. Owens, got a telegram for you. Came in last night. Here it is. It came up from Richardson."

Jed took the telegram and shoved it into his shirt pocket.

"Might want to read it, Mr. Owens. Probably want to reply."

"Maybe later. Right now I want two tickets east as far as I need to go to catch a train going south west for Richardson in Texas."

"That's right. You'll have to go by the track joining up to the next station. I can only give you tickets that far and then you get your tickets there to go on to Richardson."

After he got the tickets, Jed hurried out and up the sidewalk far enough so the agent wouldn't see then he whipped the telegram from his pocket. It was what he feared but he had ten days, well, nine now but he'd get there before that foreclosure was final. But what was he to do then anyway. He had the tickets and he might as well take Stan along. Ben said he had some money at the bank. It would likely cover their expenses.

He met his father as he was coming out of the hotel.

"Jed, you're lookin' kind of serious. Get that telegram you been expecting?"

"Yes, Papa, and it's just like I figured. The bank foreclosed on the mortgage and they want the whole amount. The only good thing is, they got ten days although I don't know how that can help."

"The bank's open now. Let's go over and see Mr. Albright. Maybe we can figure something out."

"Good morning, Ben ... Jed. I guess you're here to finish up that bit of business you set up last month. I'm glad you could give me some time on that. The bank doesn't carry a lot of money most times and it would have left us pretty short if you hadn't let me in on what you were planning. I'll just get the papers and have the staff count out the money."

"I don't reckon Jed will want to carry that much cash along. He's headin' for Texas this afternoon. Probably a thousand dollars and a bank draft for the rest. Does your bank have a branch in a town called Richardson?"

"Sure, I know the place. I'll get the staff started on that now. Jed, what are you figuring on doing in Texas? Got something in mind?"

"Had me a foreman's job when I left down there and I figured I might work myself into a share of the profits somehow."

"What he means, Mr. Albright, he's had a telegram sayin' the bank has put a foreclosure on the ranch and he's frettin' about what might happen."

"How much is the mortgage on the place. Do you know?"

"It's eleven thousand which from what I saw is about a quarter of what it's worth."

"Well, I'd say you're in a good position to buy in right now. You've got the money right here and we could send a telegram and get our bank in Richardson to clear the mortgage today. As long as I'm willing to guarantee that the money's coming through in the next few days, they'd do that for me."

"It's not that simple, Mr. Albright. Until I get a chance to speak to the owner and get the go ahead on everything, I can't just step in and take charge."

"What Jed means is the ranch is owned by a young lady and my daughter Rose, she says Jed's been smitten. That's why he's in such a hurry to get back down there."

"Your father and I have both been through the same thing in years past so we know there's no fatherly advice that will help."

One of the tellers came in and placed some papers and money on the desk.

"Okay now Jed, here's a thousand dollars in cash and this is a bank draft made out to you. It's only good at the Richardson Branch of Wells Fargo so it's pretty safe to carry and it won't be too bulky. You just sign here and that old account will be closed out. I have to thank you, Ben for leaving it with us so long. It's definitely made some money for us over these past thirty years."

When Jed picked up the bank draft, he couldn't believe what he was seeing. The amount was for twenty thousand one hundred and twenty three dollars and a few cents. He had no idea that such an amount would be there.

After they left the bank, he turned to his father.

"Papa, you can't be givin' me so much. You've got to think of yourself. You and Del could have that place buzzing by next spring."

"Yes. Or I could just keep the money and move into a boarding house somewhere and live out my years. What I've done is what is right. I've invested my money in my son and I'm sure it will multiply far faster there than in any bank. Might even raise me a crop of grand kids down there in Texas. Let's head for the cafe and have us a coffee."

When they got to the cafe, Stan was seated at a table so they joined him.

"You been up to the livery, Jed?"

"Nope. Just been to the station and the bank."

"I just came from there. Lots of interest in those last six bulls. Might be a good idea to auction them off with a hundred and thirty dollar minimum price."

"Let's give them a bit of time to get anxious then we'll stroll up. If someone's decided to take them, we'll let them go for what we asked this morning. No need to make bad feelings."

"Sure would be interesting to bring a carload of those Herefords up here in a couple of years when those bull's offspring start puttin' on weight from this Wyoming grass."

When they got back to the livery, Charlie had sorted everything out and he had gotten a promise that the heifers would be delivered out to Del's place."

"Charlie, you're a wonder. We should give you a discount on your bull."

"Now, Jed, I just did it 'cause I couldn't help myself. It's the horse trader in me."

"Anyway, you sure been a help. Join us at Mae's for lunch at noon. At least let me buy you lunch."

"Well, that you can do and I'll have a second helpin' of Mae's apple pie, too."

"Still talkin' your way into something extra, Charlie? You're right, you can't help yourself."

When they left the livery, they went out by the back door. Ben was taken aback by what he saw. Standing by a post at the corral was a picture he'd seen thirty years before. It looked like John Benson, Holly's father, although it couldn't be him. This fellow was probably twenty-five yet he had the height, the long arms and bib overalls and an old felt hat turned down all the way around.

"Come along, Jed. I think we've found a relative we should meet."

Ben couldn't help asking the question that came to his lips when they got to the corral and were standing in front of the fellow.

"You a Benson?"

"Yep."

"John's boy?"

"Yep."

"What's the first name?"

"Jack."

"Well, Jack, I'm Ben Owens. I was married to your sister, Holly. This is our son, Jed."

"Yeah, got word a while back Holly was dead. Ma and Pa they was already gone by that time."

"We were about to go for lunch. Why don't you join us?"

"Reckon not. Got me some grub down by the creek."

"This is sort of a special occasion, Jack. Jed here, he's headin' way down to Texas this afternoon and a few friends are sending him off. Sort of a party at my cost. We'd sure like for you to join us."

"I guess I could if you don't mind payin'. Been tryin' to get by till I find a job."

"Let's go now. You can bring Jed and me up on the news from Trails End."

"Can't tell you much about the present. I've been travellin' some these past three months. Left Simon and John at the old place. The rest are all married and scattered."

"Your Ma wrote one time that there were fifteen of you kids. Were you the last?"

"Yep. The runt of the litter, Pa called me. Skinny I was, always skinny. Just like Pa, I guess."

The five of them sat down and had Mae bring them coffee while they waited for Charlie to show up. Jed could tell that Ben was carefully asking Jack out but for what purpose. Maybe his father was just interested in finding out all he could about Holly's family.

Charlie showed up so they ordered. They all started eating and things got quiet. Finally, Ben revealed what all the questions were about.

"You needin' a job for a month or so, Jack?"

"I'll take most anything right now. Me and the dog are runnin' on short rations."

"You got a dog? Where is he, or is it a her?"

"It's a he and he's down by the creek lookin' out for my

camp."

"We could use an extra man out at Del and Rose's place. I told Del I might bring a man back with me. Got lots of different chores to do between now and winter. You interested?"

"What about the dog? I reckon likely he'll follow along ... been with me now most of the summer."

"Well, Del and Rose haven't any dog so we don't have to worry about a dog fight. How is he around farm animals, chickens and pigs, things like that?"

"I reckon he'll be all right. He's pretty smart in knowin' what I want him to do and he's an outdoors dog. Too big to be anything else."

"I'll be pullin' out from the livery stable before sun-up tomorrow. I've got those two bulls to take along and we'll have to camp out overnight. I'll be glad to have you along. I don't know how those bulls will act."

"Don't you worry, Mr Owens. Old Rufe, he'll put them in their place."

"That's your dogs name, Rufe?"

"Yep, that's what he says his name is. Showed up by my campfire one night and sat down while I was cookin' a rabbit. He helped me clean up that rabbit along with a biscuit apiece, then I asked him what his name was and he said Rufe. Not woof, but Rufe so I called him Rufe. Been with me ever since. I can't rightly say he belongs to me. He's more like a friend. I surely appreciate the job, Mr. Owens and I'll be there to help you with those bulls. Won't be no trouble for Rufe."

"Okay, Jack but stop the Mr. Owens. The name is Ben. Your my brother-in-law, part of the family."

At three that afternoon, Ben, Jed and Stan moved their baggage down to the station with the saddle and bedrolls. They had enough that it would have to go in the baggage car.

While they were waiting, Jed sent a telegram to Richardson in care of the Pritchard Ranch. That way anyone from the ranch could pick it up. He just said he'd be there in approximately four days. He had just received confirmation the message was received when the train came to a stop outside.

He checked a railroad map on the wall and found he would have to go to Omaha before they could turn south and west again.

"You take care, Papa and maybe I'll see you come spring. I'll write and let you know how things turn out. I know you'll be worried."

Ben threw his arms around Jed.

"Look out for yourself, Jed. I sure hate to see you go but it's for the best. Stan, you look out for him."

"I'll do what I can, Ben and it was nice workin' for you. Give my best to Del and Rose."

"I guess we need to get our gear stowed, Papa so we'll say goodby for now."

As Ben walked back to the hotel, he had tears in his eyes but he knew everything had been done for the best. Tomorrow, he had to get that corn sheller loaded onto the wagon and then hitch those two bulls to the tail end and head for Del's place. He hoped young Jack showed up. He sure could use the company and the help going home.

Chapter 9

The train journey was uneventful for Jed and Stan going east. In Omaha, they bought tickets and stowed their gear at the station while they waited for the Westbound going to Richardson.

They decided to have a good meal and went looking for a busy restaurant along front street. When they found what they were looking for, they located a table and ordered.

After the waitress had taken their order and left, Stan asked, "Jed, what do you think we'll run into down there?"

"I've been thinkin' about that and I figure whoever started this foreclosure thing is probably going to know I'm coming. That railroad agent, he's going to see the telegram I sent and he's going to try and sell it. I know he's already sold information to that Artie Smith I had the run in with."

"What do you figure that banker's going to do?"

"If he figured I might be bringin' money with me, he might try getting it away from me before I get a chance to fix things and I can't do anything in town till I see the owner of the ranch. She's made an offer of a partnership but she'll be expectin' to come to terms on that before she accepts money from me."

"It ain't likely a banker will get mixed up in gun play."

"No, but he could just tell some characters that I'm coming

and have them remove that money from my person. Does that sound about right?"

"Sure does. What are we going to do about it?"

"I'm thinkin' that before we reach Richardson, I'll give you the bank draft and what money I have except pocket money. When we get to the station, you go out one end of the car and I'll go out the other. No one knows you're with me. Before we get there, I'll pay the porter to send our luggage to the nearest hotel. That way, we'll be free to do what ever needs doing.

"You keep an eye on me. Get me out of trouble, if need be. I'm sure they'll have a good description of me. I can't be easily missed with my height and all. If I'm going to be waylaid, I hope it'll be first thing while our senses are sharp and we're expecting it."

"You going armed?"

"No. I don't want them getting gun happy and thinking I'm too dangerous to approach. You take my gun along with yours."

"I think you've got it figured straight. Let's hope it all works out."

By the time they finished their meal, it was time to head back to the station to catch the West bound. They were making better time than Jed had expected and that might throw off any plans to high jack them at the station as he had said in the telegram that he'd be four or five days before he arrived. But he couldn't depend on that if the banker was getting information from that agent, he might also find out the shortest possible time for Jed to get there from Cheyenne.

Amos Mason had made his trip out to Artie Smith's place for nothing. The only one there was the old Mexican cook and he would probably leave when supplies ran out. Artie's two men had left right after Artie got himself shot and had taken whatever they could pack onto two spare horses. When you're a man like Artie Smith you can't expect loyal help.

113

The only thing he could think of that he might do was stop at the doctor's place and have a chat with Artie. Maybe he'd be grateful enough that if Amos dropped by to tell him about his so called help, he might tell him where he could find a good man or two who would take on the job of robbing the Owens man when he came in on the train. It had to be done right away before Owens had a chance to do something with the money.

When he got to the doctors house, he met the doctor leaving with his bag in his hand.

"Good morning, Doc. How's Artie Smith doing?"

"He's doing good enough to complain about everything under the sun. Got me and the Missus about crazy."

"I just came from Artie's place. There isn't anyone there except that old Mexican who does the cooking. He told me the hired hands left the day Artie got shot. I hate to bring bad news to a sick man but I figure he better know."

"Well, go on in. The Missus will be glad to have someone to keep him busy for awhile."

Amos knocked on the door and when the doctor's wife answered, he explained to her why he was there. She smiled and thanked him for dropping in and said Artie could sure use some company. Now that he was out of danger, he was a little restless.

"You go on in. He's in the room to the right. I'll be back in the kitchen and if you need anything, you'll have to come and get me."

"Okay, but I probably won't be here long. I've got to get back to the bank, you know."

Amos left her then and walked into Artie's room. Artie was strapped to a board with his right side immobile.

When he saw Amos, he looked at him with suspicion. Why was the banker here, he didn't owe the Cattleman's Bank anything, didn't even do business there.

"I suppose you're wondering why I'm here, Artie. Well, it's

a matter that benefits us both so hear me out before you say anything. First off, I rode out to your place before I came here. I had a proposition for those two men of yours. I have to tell you, Artie there isn't anyone there except that Mexican cook. He told me your men left there with pack horses loaded down the same day you got shot."

"I might have known I couldn't count on those two. What about my stock?"

"Turned out to pasture. I guess they'll be all right for awhile. What I came to see you about, Artie, concerns that jasper who shot you. He left here with those bulls a week ago. Now he's on his way back and rumor has it, he'll be carrying some serious money. I thought you might know some boys who would relieve him of it."

"I might, Amos, I might. But what concern is that of yours?"

"I know, Artie that you've had your mind set on that Pritchard place. You can't seriously think you'll get it now and my bank has just foreclosed. Miss Pritchard has seven more days then the bank takes everything but if this Owens gets here with enough money, he's been offered a partnership."

Artie started swearing and Amos had to wait a few minutes for him to calm down before he could continue.

"Now, Artie, I don't want any of the money this Owens is carrying and you can make the deal with whatever men you might contact and leave me out of it completely."

"How come you didn't foreclose before, Amos?"

"I knew you were interested, Artie and in more than just the property. I thought I'd give you time to try your hand. It didn't matter where the bank got it's money. It could get it from you or foreclose. Now you're in no condition to do me any good on that line. I had no choice but to foreclose."

"I reckon I might know a couple of boys who might be interested but you'll have to find me a messenger then your part will be finished. Try and find old Petey. He's probably at the bar on the east end of town. Just tell him I've got an errand worth a dollar to him."

"Okay, Artie. Now one thing I found out is that Owens should be here within the next three days on a Westbound train. You might have to keep a close watch on the station at train time."

"You just leave that to me, Amos. My boys will get a schedule at the station and I can give them boys a better description than anybody else around here, seein' as I saw him out a gun barrel. How much you figure he'll have on him?"

"I can't say exactly but the mortgage is eleven thousand and there isn't much sense of him coming down here with less than that. This Pritchard woman has offered him a share in the ranch if this mortgage can be settled. Now I'd better get back to the bank. Sorry about the shoulder, Artie."

"Be seein' you, Amos."

Amos did not like the sound of that. He was already thinking he had just made a pact with the devil.

He found Petey at the bar and gave him the message that Artie had an errand for him that could earn him a dollar. Amos headed back to the bank feeling that he hadn't looked after the problem well enough but not knowing what else to do.

When Petey arrived at the Doctor's house, the Missus was going to turn him away but Artie had been listening for him to arrive and he hollered for her to let him in.

"Let Petey in here. I need him to run an errand. He'll be gone in two minutes. I got business needs doin' and I can't do it myself, laying here strapped up like a mummy."

"Well, I'll tell you, Mr. Smith, you're not going to run this house like an office. If you've got a friend or two who want to visit, that's fine but I don't want every drunk in town running through my house."

"Now don't get your hair in a tangle. Old Petey, he ain't drunk this early in the day and the only other visitor I had was the banker, Amos Mason. I'd think you'd be honored to have such company as he."

"I could do without that man in my house, too. The way he had the Sheriff foreclose on that Pritchard girl, not waiting till she sold her cattle and all. Anyways, here's old Petey. Tell him what you need him to do and send him along on his way."

"If you'll just go back to your bakin' and give me and Petey some privacy, I'll get him out of your way pretty quick."

As soon as she left the room, Artie beckoned Petey close to the bed.

"You know old Lafe and Lyle Barker, Petey?"

"Sure, Artie. Sure."

"They still comin' into town most days?"

"Yeah, I see them most days. Not very friendly towards me though. Won't buy old Petey a drink."

"You find them, Petey and you send them to see me. Just one or the other. I don't want to get the Doc's Missus any more upset. You think you could do that, Petey?"

"Mr. Mason, he said you'd give me a dollar."

"I sure will Petey but promise me before you start buyin' booze you'll find one or the other of them Bartons and tell him I want to see him. Alright?"

"Sure, Artie. I'll do that."

After Petey left with the dollar clutched in his hand, Artie cursed himself for being so helpless, laying there in bed trusting to a drunken bum to do his business for him but he needed someone who could carry a message and then forget it after he got drunk and sobered up. If things worked out right and that Owens wound up dead, he didn't want a trail leading back to him and it wouldn't take much for someone to get the idea.

117

About two o'clock, Lyle Barton showed up. The doctor's wife showed him in and she had a scowl on her face. Artie was smart enough to realize he had better slow up the foot traffic around there or he'd be back at the ranch with just the Mexican cook, if he hadn't already left. And maybe he'd be without that pain killer the Doctor gave him.

"Sit down, Lyle. I got a proposition for you. You know the guy that winged me and put me in bed here? Have you seen him?"

"Got a look at him that day as he came from the Sheriff's office."

"Well, if you've seen him once, you ain't likely to forget him. Now I got from a source that he's coming back to town in the next two or three days and he's supposed to be carryin' a fair amount of cash. I'd like for you and Lafe to relieve him of his cash and leave his body in some alley. I don't want any of the money. I just want the satisfaction of knowing he's paid for putting me here in this bed.

"There is one more thing we might do for each other. My place out west of town, I've gotten word my boys took off with a pack horse each and you can bet they took anything that wasn't fastened too tight. Why don't you and Lafe bunk out there and look out for the place. You'll have to lay in some grub. If you get that old Mex cook a bottle or two, he'll probably stay around and get your meals."

"That sounds alright, Artie. Me and Lafe, we been spendin' too much money in them damn bars. Money don't seem to last like it used to. What if this Owens don't have any money on him like your source says?"

"I can't guarantee he will, Lyle but it ain't likely he'd be coming back down here from Cheyenne broke when that Pritchard woman needs eleven thousand dollars to get her place from foreclosure and she's offered him a chance at a partnership. I'll tell you what, Lyle, if you take care of that Owens for me and his pockets turn up empty, I'll give you boys five hundred out of my own pocket."

"That's generous of you, Artie. Me and Lafe, we'll move our gear over to your place and no one will be stealin' your stuff while you're in here. I'd best be goin' and find Lafe and get the train times. Rest easy, Artie. We'll take care of this Owens for you."

It was dark when the train arrived in Richardson but the platform was well lit. Stan and Jed had already parted so that no one would see them together through the windows. Jed found the Porter and paid him to have someone take their baggage to the nearest hotel. He left by the west end of the coach and Stan headed for the east end.

Almost as soon as Jed left the steps, he spotted two men loitering on the station platform. He was quite sure Stan would see them, too so he sauntered by in front of them and headed for the nearest street going uptown.

He turned his head enough to see Stan hanging back by the train steps. Soon after, he heard footsteps behind him on the boardwalk and two men hurrying. He just kept walking. He would have to trust that Stan could get him out of the fix after the men made their play.

He hadn't gone a hundred feet when they caught up and one jammed a gun in his ribs.

"Hold it, Owens. We'd like the money you're carrying."

"You won't get much, maybe ten or eleven dollars."

"Is that so. Well, we'd better give you a good search. Let's go into this alley here, check you out real good."

"Okay, but I think you boys got some bad information. Cowboys like me, we don't go around with much money."

"Well, maybe you ain't got money on you but when we get through with you, you'll be worth five hundred to us anyway."

When they got to the end of the alley, Jed turned around and faced the two of them. He could see Stan's form coming

119

up behind them.

"You boys are going to be in trouble if you fire those guns in here. The Marshall, he don't like gunshots in his town."

"Oh, I think we can be quieter than that. Ain't nobody going to know what happened before tomorrow and we won't be anywhere around. Now you start gettin' out of them clothes. I figure you got money on you somewhere's and we'll just take your clothes along with us."

Just when Jed reached for his belt buckle, Stan came down with both hands, striking the butt of a gun to each of their heads. Both of them crumpled to the ground.

"Stan, that was close. Those boys were paid to do away with me right here in this alley."

"Yeah, I heard most of what they said. Who do you reckon paid them, this Smith fellow?"

"I'd say yes but maybe he was a go between for that banker. For sure he's mixed up in it somehow."

"What are we going to do with these boys? They'll probably be after you again."

"Let's see if we can find some identification on them."

"Here, I've found a purse on this one. Most likely if he's carrying any information like that, it will be in here."

"If there's any money there, leave it and we'll get out of here before someone comes along."

When they got to the hotel, Jed got Stan to sign them into a room then he asked if the hotel had a safe.

"Got a small one back there. What you got so valuable, cowboy?"

"Nothin' that's any good to anyone except me but I don't want to lose it."

Stan pulled out the envelope containing the bank draft and they watched as the clerk locked it up then they loaded up their gear and headed for their room.

When they got to their room, they lit the lamp and locked the door and then propped a chair under the knob.

"Here's your gun, Jed. Lucky you gave it to me or I'd have had to take those boys one at a time."

"Guess they got a bit careless with me not even armed but they sure were determined I wasn't going out of that alley alive."

Lyle and Lafe started moving and groaning about the same time. After some effort, they both sat up.

"What in hell happened, Lyle?"

"I ain't sure and I can't think too good right now."

"You reckon he had someone guardin' him?"

"I didn't see anyone."

"Neither did I but I got me a notion we was set up somehow."

"Light a match and see if our guns and stuff are here."

"What's this money doin' laying here?"

"I don't know, Lafe. It ain't much but it's enough to get us a drink to clear the cobwebs. Hey, my purse is gone. That's my own dang money."

"Why would they take your purse? Anything in it besides money?"

"No, I don't think so."

"Nothin' to identify you to the Marshall?"

"Nope."

"Then let's get out of here and find a drink and clear our heads. We sure made a mess of this job but maybe we can think of another way to come at it."

They staggered down the street till they came to the first watering hole. They entered, got a bottle and two glasses and seated themselves at the farthest table.

"You figure that Owens was tipped off, Lafe?"

"I don't think so. I figure he smelled a rat in the works from something that happened on his first trip down here and he came prepared. It's obvious he had help with him on that train."

"Artie sure ain't going to like it with Owens gettin' away."

"Oh, we can still collect that five hundred from Artie later and we got a score to settle ourselves now. Don't be forgettin' the lumps we got on our heads."

"What about the money he was supposed to be carrying? You figure somebody had that all wrong?"

"I figure he might have given it to the dude that hit us on the head or he could of sent it some other way, being as how he figured out what might happen at the station."

"Where do you figure they went to?"

"It ain't likely they went too far, gettin' in this time of night."

"Maybe we should check the hotels. See if they got this Owens on the register."

"That's an idea. We'll just sit here and think about it while things quiet down inside my head."

After they had another drink, Lafe started laying out what he thought happened.

"I figure those boys are in a hotel right close to the station. They didn't get off with any luggage so they must have hired someone to take it somewhere for them. That train pulled out just while we were walkin' down the street here."

"What you figure then, Lafe. Is there anything we can do tonight?"

"Might be. I've been thinkin' that if Owens was carrying anything valuable, he'd be certain to put it somewhere safe, at least for tonight. When I think of safe now I recollect most hotels have a safe for the travellers to leave stuff in. What say we stroll by some of those hotels closest to the station. What do you think, Lyle. That make sense?"

"It does but how are we gonna find him if we don't know what to look for?"

"We'll just kind of ask the clerk if that long drink of water is stayin' there. Nobody's going to miss someone that tall."

"What you figure we should do if we find where he's at?"

"I don't figure we should try to even the score for these sore heads tonight. They'll be safely locked inside their room. We'll see if we can find what he might of been carrying that was so valuable. Let's start with the hotel closest to the station."

When they approached the desk, Lafe just asked the clerk right quick, "You got a feller stayin' here who might have to duck coming through that door? Maybe came in a couple of hours ago?"

"You friends of his?"

"You might say we'd like to be real close with him."

"He's in room ten at the front, him and his friend."

"I don't suppose he might have left something with you for safe keeping? We was supposed to pick something up here at the desk, something he was leaving here for us."

"No, he never left anything to give you boys. Sorry."

"But he did leave something with you didn't he, something to put in that little safe there?"

"Well, yes but I can't give it to you on your say so."

 Lafe pulled his gun.

"Maybe we could change your mind about that. Ain't no reason for you to get hurt. It's not your money."

"Well, Mister, if it's money you're looking for, you might as well back out of here. It's something in an envelope and he said it was no good to anyone but him. I remember that."

"You just go ahead and open that safe and pass it over and you won't get hurt."

The clerk opened the safe and passed the envelope over.

"Can't be anything in there to go to this much trouble over."

"What are we going to do with him, Lafe? Can't leave him to sound the alarm. We need time to study on this."

"You're right, Lyle. Take him into the office and tie him up and stuff something in his mouth."

Lyle took the clerk back to the office and yanked the rope

off the window curtain and tied the clerk hand and foot. Then he gagged him. When he had this done, it came to him that the clerk might raise enough racket with his bound feet to get attention although everybody seemed to be in their rooms for the night. He whipped out his gun and slammed the clerk on top of the head. When he came back out to the desk, Lafe had the envelope open and the bank draft in his hand.

"Know what I got here, Lyle? I got us a bank draft for over twenty thousand dollars! You ever had a bank draft, Lyle?"

"Not me personal but I seen a feller once had one for a herd of cattle he sold. He had to present it at the bank, personal like. Had to prove who he was and everything."

"You sayin' this here ain't no good to you and me?"

"I can't see how. What bank is it writ on?"

"The Wells Fargo here in town."

"Then it ain't no good for you and me. You can be sure there's somebody in that bank that knows us and anyway that Owens feller, he's going to go to that bank first thing and tell them this things been stole."

"What are you saying, Lyle that we should put it back or something?"

"I'm saying we should get the hell outta here and then figure if there's any way we can make some money with this thing. If it's valuable to Owens to have it then it's valuable to someone else that he don't have it. Let's get out of here before someone comes."

They went back to the same bar where they were before and occupied the same table.

"What do you think, Lyle?"

"I think one of us needs to see Artie again. I figure he can tell us where we might trade this thing for some cash."

"Come morning, Lafe, the Marshals going to be on the lookout for you and me. When the clerk starts telling his story, there's no way we ain't going to be tagged for the boys who robbed that safe and if that Owens sees us, he'll probably come a runnin' with his gun out. Now I don't mind meeting up with him but at my own time. You know what I mean?"

"He sure did take care of Artie pretty slick. I think we've got to get out of town and move out to Artie's place but somehow we got to get some grub."

"We don't have much time, Lafe. Maybe we should help ourselves over at the mercantile and then ride on out to Artie's."

"Well, I like the first part of your idea. We load up out behind that store then you head for Artie's place. I'll stay hid here in town till I get a chance to talk to Artie and find out who might pay for this here bank draft."

"Ain't going to be nobody pay for that thing. It ain't no good to anybody."

"It's still good to Owens. Somebody in this town went to some trouble to relieve him of it. Might be worth while to buy it off us if I kind of threatened to put it back in Owens hands. Could be worth a thousand, I'm thinking."

"Let's get goin' before something breaks loose and they start lookin' for us."

They left the bar and brought their horses around behind the store. A few minutes later they had the back door open.

"You remember where stuff is in there, Lyle? We can't have much light, the Marshal might take a walk by."

"I can get to the canned goods alright. I'll load a sack of them and then look around. You come in and watch the street through the front. That way, I can light a match now and again."

"We'll make sure we got lots. No way of knowing when it'll be safe to show ourselves again. Load both horses and take mine with you, too. I'll borrow one at the hitch rail when I'm ready to leave. It's best if both our horses are gone anyway. Maybe no one will look too hard for us tomorrow."

"Where you going to stay tonight, Lafe?"

"I'm thinkin' that little barn behind the doctors house. Must be a bit of hay there I can sleep on. Somehow tomorrow, I got to get to Artie and find out who needs this bank draft."

"I'm all set, Lafe. Give me a hand with these sacks and if you can get the chance tomorrow, you bring us out something to drink. Might be awhile before we can show ourselves."

"Might not be able to show ourselves in this town ever again if that Marshal finds out what all we been up to."

"Do you think Owens will make a report? He could have just turned us in last night."

"I'm thinkin' he figured he came out on top last night and he just let it stand at that but as soon as that clerk raises the alarm and tells his story, we ain't going to be safe around here, especially if we're together. Not many sets of twins roamin' the streets."

"Okay, I'll head out to Artie's and get squared away with that Mex cook of his. Maybe if we could get him a bit to drink, we could keep him around to cook for us."

"Sure, Lyle. Promise him whatever it takes and tell him Artie is sending us out to look after things till he's better."

Chapter 10

Jed and Stan woke early the next morning. They washed up and headed down stairs looking for some breakfast. As they came to the desk, there was no sign of anyone but before they got out of earshot, they heard some banging on the office door so they turned back.

Jed knocked on the door.

"What's going on in there?"

More banging from inside.

"Sounds like trouble, Stan. Let's see if we can get this door open."

When Jed turned the knob, the door started to open then it was stopped by some obstruction. Then there was a shuffling noise and the door opened further. Now Jed could get his head around the edge and he could see the clerk bound and gagged, laying just inside the door.

Gradually, they got the door fully open and stepped inside. The first thing Jed did was pull the gag loose so the man could breath properly. Then he set to work to loosen his hands and feet.

As soon as the gag was out, the clerk started to explain what happened.

"Two men, twins I think, came in and asked about you, Mr. Owens. Soon as they found out you were stayin' here, they wanted to know if you left anything in the safe. Said they was to pick it up here. I told them I couldn't just pass it over without your say so and I guess that was a mistake 'cause then they knew you had left something in the safe.

"They pulled guns and told me to open up. I remembered you saying whatever it was, it was useless to anyone but you and I told them that but it didn't stop them. They made me open up and they took the envelope. Then one of them brought me in here and tied me up. I thought that was all he would do but he hit me over the head before he left.

"I was out, I don't know how long. Then I worked my way to the door, played myself out tryin' to get someone's attention. Then I heard you two walk by and banged my feet again. Sure feels good to get them ropes off. I'm sorry about your envelope but I didn't have much choice."

"How did they know you'd put that bank draft in the safe, Jed?"

"Probably just some good guessing. After all, we had a narrow escape last night because I had given it to you before we came off the train. I guess they took the time to figure the most logical thing."

"What are you going to do, now?"

"As soon as the clerk gets washed up and able to walk proper, I suppose we should all go down to the Marshal's office and make a report."

"How come you didn't make a report last night about what happened to us?"

"The Marshal here doesn't like paper work and us being strangers in town, we might have rubbed him the wrong way and wound up in jail ourselves and we can't waste time. We've got to get out to the Pritchard place and get things settled but now we've got this clerk here who's been assaulted so we better go along with him and tell the whole story."

When they got to the Marshal's office, there was a deputy on duty.

"What can I do for you, gentlemen? Good morning, Lennie. What happened to you? These men give you a hard time."

"No, Gary. Two men robbed the safe at the hotel and took an envelope that Mr. Owens left there for safe keeping."

"Owens? You're the man who had the shoot out with Artie Smith last week."

"Yeah, that was me."

"Thought I heard you went back north."

"I did and now I'm back. Now can you start taking down what we tell you. First off, when I got off the train last evening, I was waylaid by two men, taken to an alley and from the way they talked, they meant to leave me there dead.

"They knew somehow that I was coming back south and they had the impression I might be carrying a large sum of money. During the trip down, I thought I would let my friend carry most of my money and a bank draft I had in an envelope. When we got off the train, my friend and I left by different doors on the coach. My friend was able to rescue me at the end of that alley and we left two men there unconscious. I hoped they would give up but they followed us to the hotel and forced Lennie to open the safe and give them the bank draft. Then they tied Lennie up and pistol whipped him."

"Do you have any names you can give me for these two men?"

"Lennie says he heard the name Lyle and that they seemed to be twins. Stan and I only saw them in dim light but I would agree they had the same build and sounded the same."

"Sure sounds to me like you tangled with the Barton twins, Lafe and Lyle. They've been around town here for the last while. I don't know where they're sleeping. You're lucky you had your friend along, Owens. Those two are pretty mean. If they're still in town, Herb will find them before the days out. He's been lookin' for a reason to put them behind bars. Everything Owens says here, Lennie, is that the way it happened?"

129

"Yeah, that's what happened at the hotel. I wasn't at the other part."

"Okay, each of you sign this sheet I wrote everything on and when Herb comes in, I guess we'll be searching the town for those boys. You got any ideas what they're up to, Mr. Owens?"

"Well, I came down here to help Miss Pritchard. She offered me a partnership if I had enough money to pay off the mortgage on her place. The only reason I can figure someone would know that I was on my way here and maybe had money on me is if that telegraph operator who took the message that was sent to me carried it to someone else who might be interested. Maybe Artie Smith is still dealing cards in the game or maybe the bank, or someone at the bank."

"That surely was a mean bit of business putting the foreclosure on that property when that Pritchard woman could have brought that mortgage right up to date in another week. That Amos Mason sure didn't make any friends around here. We'll check Artie out and maybe we should have a chat down at the station and see who was on duty when that message went up to you in Cheyenne."

"I've still got the message here. It might be of help to you. I certainly don't need it anymore."

"It could be a big help. It's got the time it was sent so there won't be any dispute about who might have been working the key when that message was sent. This person, Ricky that signed here, do you know who that is?"

"Sure, he was acting foreman out at the ranch."

"Then he could identify who sent the message."

"Most likely, yes."

"Then I'm sure Herb will rout him out and find who he peddled that information to. You going to be able to help that Pritchard woman now that they've stolen your bank draft?"

"Well, I don't see how I can do much but I'm sure going to hang around and see what takes place in the next few days."

130

"I wish you luck, Mr. Owens and if I were you I wouldn't be out after dark."

"We'll leave you now Deputy Winslow and thanks for your concern."

"How are you feeling, Lennie. Could you eat some breakfast?"

"I sure could go for some coffee anyhow and then I'll see how that sets on my stomach."

"Then let's head for that cafe across the street. When we get seated, you can tell us how to get to the Wells Fargo Bank from here."

After they had their breakfast, they parted with the hotel clerk and made their way to the bank. It had just opened. Jed asked one of the tellers if he could see the manager. He was beckoned into the office after a brief wait.

"Mr. Owens, I'm Jim Westgate. How can I help you?"

Jed laid out his problem and Westgate thought about it for a few minutes.

"There's no way anyone else can use that bank draft now that we know about it. Mr. Albright wrote it so that it was only good at this particular branch and seeing as it was for a fair amount, he sent us a telegram that you might require a sizable amount right away so we would be ready. I'll alert the staff in case someone should pass himself off as you. What we need then is a new bank draft from Cheyenne. It would have to come by mail and it might take some days. I take it your time to wait is limited?"

"That's right. I surely would like to clear this thing up with the Pritchard mortgage. I'm sure things are hanging out there that should be done."

"I'll tell you what I'll do, Mr. Owens. I'll give you a personal loan for one month covered by this bank draft that's coming down from Cheyenne. We'll put the money right into your account which we will open before you leave here. It will take maybe five minutes. How would that be?"

"Mr. Westgate, I can't thank you enough. Now there's one more thing I need. That's the name of an able and honest lawyer here in town. I'm going to have him look out for this mortgage thing and maybe later make out some partnership papers. So if you could tell me of someone and give me directions, it sure would be helpful."

"I'd suggest Otis Sinclair. He's my personal lawyer and he was recommended to me when I was transferred here to Richardson ten years ago and I haven't had any complaints. His office is three blocks down east and on the same side of the street as the bank. You can't miss it. Is there anything else I can help you with?"

"No, I've had my mind relieved of all it's problems for now, Mr. Westgate. You've been more that helpful."

"I'm glad you brought your problems here, Mr. Owens. When this mortgage is cleared up, you might let it be known how helpful Wells Fargo has been. Not many people around here like how the Cattleman's Bank conducted themselves."

Jed and Stan left the bank and went down the street to the lawyers office. When he told them he was referred by Mr. Westgate, he got right in. Jed came right to the first issue, the mortgage that was due in three days.

"I'm going to leave you with twelve thousand dollars and on Friday before three o'clock, I want you to go to the Cattleman's Bank and pay out that mortgage."

"I can't do that without Ellen Pritchard's consent, Mr. Owens. She might not want to be indebted to you in any way."

"I'll have her come in before that time but I've had trouble here in town and I might be taken out of the picture, either temporarily or permanently. Someone is trying to keep me from getting that foreclosure thing settled. But no matter what happens to me, you pay that mortgage. Hopefully, Miss Ellen and I will come to terms on a partnership agreement and if things don't get tangled up, we will be in to conclude that part of the business."

"Okay, Mr. Owens but make sure Miss Pritchard gets in to sign whatever papers that are necessary so I can act on her behalf. Otherwise, the Cattleman's Bank could refuse to take the money."

"There's enough money there to pay the mortgage and any charges they might add on and maybe enough for your fees. Somebody will see that is taken care of, either myself or Miss Ellen."

"Okay, Mr. Owens. I'll get it done for you."

When Jed went out to the sidewalk where Stan was waiting, he found him looking the town over.

"What do you think of the town, Stan?"

"Seems to have most everything a man might need. How did you make out?"

"I've got everything done that I can do here in town. We'd better get a couple of horses and head out for the ranch."

At the livery, the owner still wanted to talk about the shootout between Artie Smith and Jed but Jed didn't add anything to the story so finally he led them out to the corral and told them to take their pick of a half dozen horses. As soon as they were saddled up, they headed out.

"There's a little place about three miles south, Stan where we'll stop for lunch. The woman who runs the place will probably fill us in on what's been goin' on at the ranch."

When they got to Sally's Cafe, there was one other horse tied up at the rail.

Inside, there were two tables occupied ... two oldsters at one and a single man at the other.

Right away, Jed decided the third man didn't belong in Breckenridge. One of the men at the other table was as Rick referred to him, old man Estey, the saddle maker and he hailed Jed.

"Mr Owens, good to see you back. What good deed you going to do us this time ... maybe get Miss Ellen out from under that foreclosure?"

"I sure would have liked to but somebody robbed me last night."

"Somebody must have known you was comin' and carryin' cash."

"Well, thank God, it wasn't cash. It was a bank draft but without it, there's not much I can do."

"Dang it, that's too bad. Come set down with us. This is Jim Queen and don't ask what he does. It would take me at least ten seconds to bring you up to speed on what all he's done today."

"Jim, this is Jed Owens that took Artie Smith down a week or two ago."

"It's good to meet you, Mr Owens. Estey's right, I don't do much. I just pile up what Estey makes these days. Most times, you'll find us in here having our coffee."

"I guess Mr Estey's told you then, maybe a few times what a fine job he did on that holster for me."

"Yeah, he did give me a hint or two that he might of had something to do with the outcome of that gun fight."

"Boys, this is Stan Murphy. I brought him down from Cheyenne with me on what will be a fools errand."

Sally came and took their order then cleaned the empty dishes from the other man's table. Jed could see that the man would have liked to stay awhile but Sally was standing waiting for his money.

After he left, Sally said, "If I'd gotten the chance, I'd have warned you that man is looking out for the bank, seeing that Miss Ellen don't move anything out. It's too bad he got such an earful."

"Well, Sally, sometimes if you listen hard like that fellow was, you hear something useful and other times if you keep your ears too wide open next to a manure spreader, you'll get them full of bullshit."

As soon as Jed's words sank in, they all had a good laugh.

"So everything you said was lies?"

"No, not everything. I did sort of get my pockets picked last night at the hotel but why don't we let that gentleman spread his news for now."

Mr Estey spoke up then.

"Owens, I like the way you work. Sure would be nice if you could get the Pritchard place going again."

After they ate lunch, he and Stan left and headed for the ranch. Estey was still asking questions as they rode away.

As they rode into the ranch yard, everyone except Miss Ellen was sitting on the verandah. By the time Jed and Stan got to the hitch rail, they were all on their feet. Ricky was the first to speak.

"Who's with you?"

"This is Stan Murphy, boys. Stan, this is Ricky Dansen, Chad Wilcox and Rolly. What in heck do they call you for a last name, Rolly?"

"Sanders, Rolander Sanders. Just call me Rolly, Stan."

"Stan worked for my father on the *Rocking O* and he decided he might like to see a bit of Texas so I told him if things worked out and I had a job, we could use him here. He don't mind gettin' his hands dirty mending stuff so I think you boys will welcome that. Is Miss Ellen to home?"

"Oh, sure. I think she's just waitin' to meet a bit more private."

"I do need to talk some with her alone so you boys get acquainted while I go see to some things."

When Jed went inside, Miss Ellen just stared at him for a minute then she spoke very formal.

"I see you've arrived safely."

"Oh sure, Miss Ellen. I'm sorry I wasn't here to see to

things like I should of been. You sort of hired me to be foreman and you should have expected better."

"Lord heavens, Jed, it wasn't your fault. I knew when you came here you'd be going back north to deliver those bulls and we had no way of knowing the bank would foreclose before we could sell that beef."

"I should have known. Rolly sort of give the picture of how things stood here - mortgage long overdue, no visits from the bank. They were just letting you get into a corner so they could close the gate. Now let's sit down and figure out what we can do about forming a partnership and if you're uncertain about anything, you call on one of the boys or the whole crew and ask their advice.

"First off, I'm not familiar with ranch values down here in Texas but I'd not put this place on the market for less than forty thousand. Now it might be worth more than that. I'd like to buy into a partnership but I can't come up with quite what I should have for an equal partnership. But I reckon the value you'd gain by having me as a partner and foreman, I think it would equal out in a year or two. I'll tell you I've got enough to pay the mortgage and maybe another nine thousand left over that I'd be willing to put in the ranch bank account to pay expenses till we get this place paying. What do you think? Maybe you should talk to Rolly and the boys."

"Jed, I'm just happy to get that mortgage paid off and things on the mend here. I don't need any time to think about it. I'll accept an equal partnership."

"Then, Miss Ellen, let's shake on it."

When Jed's hand touched hers, Ellen felt something that she hadn't felt in all her twenty-five years and she thought, *why can't we have a full partnership in every sense.* But that was a silly thought to come into a business deal like this.

"Maybe we should let the boys in on this, Miss Ellen. There sure was somber faces out there when I rode in."

They moved together out through the door. All had gone

quiet on the verandah. Miss Ellen opened the conversation first.

"Boys, Jed has made me an offer to be a full partner in the ranch. The mortgage will be paid in full with some money left over for expenses. With the backup of cattle that we have on hand ready to ship, we should be in good shape by wintertime. Now I'll let Jed speak."

"First off, I want to caution you boys to keep this quiet. Somebody is determined that this place go on a mortgage sale, most likely someone at the bank, not necessarily the bank itself. I've made arrangements in town for the mortgage to be paid on Friday. All it needs is for Miss Ellen to sign a paper so the lawyer can act on her behalf. We could do it today but I've decided for the next three days I'm going to try and find out who's behind all the moves against this place.

"It could still be Artie Smith pulling strings. At least I know he's tryin' to get back at me for what I did to his shoulder. Just watch what you say and don't ride alone for a few days. We can't be sure who might be in danger. One thing's for sure, Miss Ellen and myself could be targets and the best thing we can do is get that paper fixed up at the lawyer's office first thing tomorrow.

"Miss Ellen, I'm sorry, I should have introduced Stan Murphy. He's sort of my side kick so I brought him along to help out here."

"Welcome, Stan. We can use the help when we get to work again. Jed will be the boss but I'm going to be boss in the kitchen till we get well enough along so we can have a cook house and a regular cook."

"I reckon us boys will agree to that, Miss Ellen. You turn out the finest grub around here."

Jed stepped in and continued.

"Tomorrow we all head to town except Rolly and his shotgun. He stays here in case anyone decides to make a move early. You'll be within your rights, Rolly to protect the place. It's Miss Ellen's till that mortgage is up. I think the rest of us will give a little show of force and protection for Miss Ellen. We don't know how far those folks might go if they figure we might put a wrench in the works. If someone was to kidnap Miss Ellen and hold her till after Friday and that mortgage foreclosure, we'd be in big trouble."

Miss Ellen turned toward the house.

"If you boys will excuse me, I'd better get something started for supper."

Chapter 11

When Doug Engals left the Cafe, he was of two minds about what to do. First, Amos Mason had told him to keep a close watch on the ranch and see that they didn't move any cattle. But then he had said if he saw anything he thought Amos should know, to ride in and report it.

He hadn't seen anything but he'd sure gotten an earful that Mr Mason would like to know about. What should he do? After some thought, he decided he'd better ride into Richardson and report what he had heard.

He arrived at the bank before it closed and Mr Mason was still in his office.

"What are you doing in town, Doug?"

"I heard some things I figured you might want to know."

"Then let's hear it. I've got an appointment."

"Well, that Owens fellow stopped at the Cafe over in Breckenridge while I was eatin' lunch. Must have been just on his way to the Pritchard place and didn't know I was working for you. Anyways, he was tellin' Mr Estey that there wasn't much he could do for the Pritchard woman because someone had stolen whatever he was carrying to help her out."

"I see. Anything else, Doug?"

"Only that he'd come down here from Cheyenne on what turned out to be a fools errand."

"I'm glad you rode in, Doug but you'd better get back. This

Owens might have something up his sleeve yet."

After Doug rode away, Amos set out for the Doctor's place. He'd gotten that little note an hour ago but he couldn't get away and he'd been sweating the whole time. Now he knew from what Doug said that some part of Artie's plan had succeeded but why did Artie need to see him. He didn't like going to the doctor's house. He and Artie had nothing in common and someone was going to start connecting the dots pretty soon. This would have to be the last time.

When he arrived and knocked, the Doctor came to the door.

"You back again, Amos?"

"Yes, Artie Smith sent word that he needed to see me. Bank business, Frank."

"Well, I'll leave you with him but don't take too long. I need to get those bandages changed. Go right on in."

Amos headed on into Artie's room and found Artie in the same position as before.

"How are you doing, Artie?"

"Not too damn good."

"I heard those boys took care of our business last night."

"I have to tell you, Amos, they ain't too happy. They wound up with sore heads and a bank draft for twenty thousand that ain't worth nothin' to them. On top of that, they had to pistol whip the clerk at the Windsor Hotel and they figure by now the Marshal knows who they are so they can't hang around town no more."

"I guess that could be a set back for them and I'm sorry to hear they didn't get any cash off Owens. It worked out okay for me. Seems Owen can't come up with the money in time for the mortgage."

"If I was you, Amos I wouldn't count on that too much. That man is pretty slick. I found out since I been in here that right hand Owens had all bandaged was only sprained.

Maybe he couldn't draw with it but he surely let everyone know he had a gun hand that was useless. Took advantage of me, he did."

"What did you want to see me for, Artie? Anything out at the ranch need looking after?"

"Well, Lyle and Lafe Barton, the boys that tackled Owens last night, they're out at my place. They need some whiskey and they need to see you, too."

"I can't see any reason why I should go out there, Artie. I'd just as soon stay away from them. You say they were identified at the hotel?"

"Amos, I don't think you're graspin' the situation those boys got themselves into last night trying to do a job for you. They didn't get a nickel and they didn't kill that damned Owens so they didn't get the five hundred I promised either. Now the boys kind of figure that bank draft is worth a thousand to somebody and they're willing to give you first offer. If you don't come through, they'll make an offer to Owens to sell it back to him for a thousand. If he needs it real bad, maybe he can scare up that thousand. What do you think, Amos? Remember, it don't matter to me. I'm just doing this for the boys so they'll get a bit for the work they put in last night."

"If you see them again, Artie, you tell them I'll be out there tomorrow afternoon. First, I'll need to find a thousand dollars."

"Oh, Amos, I'm sure the bank will loan you that much just on your good name."

"I had better get back. I like to be there when the bank closes. I hope this is the last time I have to come here."

"Just remember when you start a deal, there's no tellin' how many times you have to ante up, Amos."

While Amos walked back to the bank, he considered all his options. He could stop right now and see how things turned out or he could take that ride out to Artie's place and see what he could do with those Barton twins. Maybe he could get them down to five hundred but he had better go prepared to pay a thousand.

The third option was to inform the Sheriff where the Bartons could be found and let justice take it's course. But then if the bank draft was found, it would be given back to Owens which would effectively stop that mortgage foreclosure because Doug had told him that Owens had come down here with all intentions of forming a partnership with the Pritchard woman.

One thing for sure, those Bartons weren't going to be happy with one bottle of whisky so he'd better start buying a bottle one at a time at different bars and damn it, he'd have to forgo the cheap stuff and buy his own brand.

One more thing bothered him. He hadn't heard anything more from that station agent. Maybe there wasn't anything to report but he would have thought that Owens or the Wells Fargo Bank would be sending a wire to Cheyenne. That bank draft could be replaced but it would have to come by mail. Most likely it would be too late. Friday was the last day. The mail didn't come in till after five o'clock and the mortgage closed at three. That agent should still be there after the bank closed. Maybe he should check with him.

He closed everything up for the night then walked down to the station and sure enough, it was the same man on duty.

"Hello, Wally. I just came by to see if there was anything going out on the wires today."

"Amos, I can't help you anymore. The Marshal was in and he as much as accused me of peddling information. Then Mr Westgate from Wells Fargo came down and he told me if he ever found out that I had betrayed any of the banks business, he'd have me before the Judge and he'd see I never operated a telegraph again. Said Wells Fargo owned enough rail stock it could have me barred. I can't help you any more, Amos."

"I guess Westgate was here to send a message to Wells Fargo in Cheyenne. Is that right, Wally?"

"I can't help you, Amos so get out of here before someone sees us talkin' and I lose my job anyhow."

"Okay, Wally. I can see you're in a bind right now. Maybe some other time."

As Amos walked back to his house, he came to the assumption that Westgate had wired Cheyenne but that didn't matter much. The mail would be too late and you couldn't wire a Bank Draft.

He decided that maybe he did owe those Barton boys a thousand. They had stopped Owens just as effectively as if they had robbed him of twenty thousand in gold. He'd better stop off and buy some whiskey for tomorrow.

In the morning, Amos went to the bank and opened up then told the staff he'd be gone a few hours. He got a thousand dollars from the safe. He'd fix that up after he got back. He went to the livery for a horse then stopped off at the house for three bottles of whiskey and headed west out of town.

As he was coming onto the main thoroughfare, he watched a buckboard with Miss Ellen and it had to be this Owens along with three riders who seemed to be an escort. Amos held back and let them all pass and then waited to see where they would go.

The buckboard stopped, as near as Amos could tell in front of Otis Sinclair's office. It might be they weren't going in there but Amos had an urge to find out. Most likely they were looking for some way to get more time on that mortgage. Amos knew there was no way that could be done but it still worried him some.

He turned his horse down a side street and tied him to a post and scurried through an alley, hoping nobody would see him. Sure enough, the trio of cowboys were hunkered down by the front wall, waiting.

One other thing came to Amos' mind then, an agreement of partnership would need a lawyer. But how could they have a partnership if the mortgage foreclosed. Again his mind wavered. Let the whole thing unwind as it would or go out to Artie's and make sure of the Bank Draft.

Maybe he was sending good money after bad but he had to keep this thing on the rails till Friday. He went back and got his horse and rode west for Artie's horse ranch.

When he got to Artie's, there didn't seem to be anyone around so finally he dismounted and knocked on the door. After awhile, an old Mexican came to the door. After some difficulty making the old man understand that he was looking for Lafe and Lyle, the Mexican pointed to a shack about fifty yards from the house.

Then he wondered why they hadn't showed themselves. Could it be that they had no idea who Artie was dealing for. Maybe he should have left it that way. He led his horse over to the shack and hollered.

"You boys want this whiskey or don't you?"

The door opened and Lyle and Lafe stepped through. This was the first Amos had seen of them. They were as alike as two peas in the same pod. They were dirty and scruffy from drinking the night before but Amos had to remind himself that they were not stupid. They were plenty crafty in their dealings, the way they figured out what Owens would do with that Bank Draft proved that.

"Artie said I might find you boys here and maybe we could do some business."

"Then I reckon he told you we didn't get one damn thing out of the dust up at the station except a worthless Bank Draft and a sore head."

"But you got to admit if Owens had been carrying cash, it

would have been the best payday you two ever had. I'll give you five hundred for that Bank Draft and you can have these three bottles of whiskey at no charge. Do we have a deal?"

"Lyle and me, we don't make deals. We say what we want and you can take it or leave it. I figure if we get in touch with this Owens, he'll take us up on it."

"He might just put the law on you."

"He'd probably try once he got the Draft back but it seems that piece of paper is pretty important between now and Friday. I kind of pieced things together from what Lyle and me heard around town that you're makin' a try at gettin' that Pritchard Ranch and this Owens might be honing in on your deal. The price is a thousand dollars in cash right now. I'm sure you didn't come all the way out here with only five hundred dollars and three bottles of whiskey hoping we might deal and take it. You're this Amos Mason we heard about in the bars. The one that won't let that Pritchard gal sell her cattle. So what do you say, Amos, you want this piece of paper?"

"Okay, don't get yourself riled. I'll pay the thousand and here's your whiskey."

"Three bottles won't do long. Lyle and me, we're big men and just sittin' here all day with nothing to do and we'll have to give that old Mex one so he'll cook for us. I think you should bring out some more tomorrow, say another three bottles."

Amos paid over the thousand dollars and Lafe gave him the Bank Draft. Then Amos told him he couldn't come back out the following day.

"Well, that's too dang bad, Amos. Then Lyle or me or both will have to ride in and get our own. Sure hope we don't get caught. I figure if Lyle and me ever get put in a cage, we'd sing like two canaries and that wouldn't be good for your little deal. After Friday, maybe things won't be so fragile but I don't think you better take that chance, Amos. You just bring us out some whiskey and we'll stay right here out of sight till you get your little deal done. Then maybe Lyle and me, we might just ride away somewheres."

After Amos left, Lyle asked Lafe why they shouldn't just saddle up right now and head out."

"Ain't no reason to hurry. That Marshal ain't going to be ridin' out here and we got lots of grub. Amos will bring some more whiskey tomorrow and if he gets that mortgage closed Friday, might be we could squeeze him for another thousand before we pull out. Besides, we promised Artie we'd look out for his place here so now let's you and me check out this particular brand of whiskey. Never had such fancy stuff before."

When Otis Sinclair had taken down all the information regarding the terms of the Partnership agreement and Jed and Miss Ellen had signed, Jed reminded him that he was to pay off the mortgage on Friday no matter what else took place between now and then. He and Miss Ellen had signed for him to act on their behalf and if something should happen to one or the other, the mortgage would still be cleared.

"Do you expect something to happen to you, Mr Owens?"

"It might, although I let it be known I had lost that Bank Draft. Then there's the possibility that they could kidnap Miss Ellen till after Friday although that would be a bit drastic. Don't say anything about our business here this morning or you could be in some danger yourself. When you go to the bank, maybe you should take the Marshal or his Deputy. It would be handy to have a witness and a little protection wouldn't hurt."

"I don't think I'll be in danger but I'll take your advice."

"Then we'll leave it in your hands, Mr Sinclair and at three o'clock on Friday, we start working cattle again."

On the way back to the ranch, Miss Ellen wanted to know

why they hadn't just paid off the mortgage today.

"I want whoever is behind this to sweat from now until the last minute and maybe we'll find out who all is behind it. That bank manager is for sure but is he acting for himself or somebody else like Artie Smith. I'm going back into town and talk to the Marshall this afternoon."

"Do you have to, Jed? I remember what you said to Mr Sinclair that we were all in danger."

"It's you more than me, Miss Ellen. Someone could hold you till after Friday and they would think they would be safe not knowing Mr Sinclair had been hired to do this business for you. Me, I'm an unknown factor but as far as they know they pulled my teeth when they took that Bank Draft. I could be in some danger from Artie Smith through those Barton twins but I don't figure they'll be around town and I'll have Stan with me."

Nothing new developed and on Friday at three o'clock, Jed had every hand and the dog working cattle toward the home place.

"What are you in such an all fired hurry for, Jed? Now that the mortgage is lifted, there's time ain't there?"

"Well, Stan, it's just that I want that overseer running for town to report that we're working cattle. It just gives me a good feeling. Don't you feel the same?"

"I surely do and those other boys have been sittin' on that porch a lot longer that we have. I reckon they appreciate this chance to earn their wages."

"Tomorrow, I've got to go to town and arrange for a buyer. Maybe there's already one hangin' around, waitin' to see if he's going to buy from the bank or Miss Ellen. Also, I need to advertise those young bulls. Could be we'd get a better price and we wouldn't have to cut them."

"It might be that buyer would take them. We must have enough for at least one, maybe two carloads. If you find a buyer in town, ask him. It sure would save us some hassle and from what I see around here, this place needs a couple of months work before winter."

On Friday night, Lyle Barton saddled up and slipped into town. The first person he saw was old Petey going from one saloon to the next. Lyle called to him from the mouth of an alley.

"Hey, Petey, you reckon you could get us a bottle if I give you some money?"

"Sure, Mister. Old Petey sure needs a drink. You give me the money, I'll get a bottle. Maybe two bottles, if you want."

"Sure, Petey. Here's some money. You go in and get us two bottles."

When Petey came back out, he was clutching two bottles to his chest.

"Them boys were sure surprised, me buying two bottles. I told them Old Petey still had friends."

"Where can we go to have a quiet drink, just you and me, Petey?"

"You just follow me. Hey, what's your name anyhow?"

"You just call me Friend, Petey."

"Sure, sure. You really are my friend now. You come around this corner here and Petey's got a nice seat where no one will bother us none."

As soon as Petey had his first drink, Lyle started asking questions about what news there was in town."

"Well, friend, you should of seen the folks at three o'clock, watchin' the road, expectin' that Owens to come riding in to pay that Pritchard woman's mortgage. Then you know what, that lawyer he comes out of his office and along comes the Marshal and they go right over to the Cattleman's Bank with just five minutes to spare and they clear that mortgage slick as a whistle."

"That's sure interesting, Petey. I expect Amos Mason was

sure surprised."

"He surely was. Some of the boys was sayin' as how Mr Westgate at the Wells Fargo Bank had come through for Mr Owens, the guy that came down here from up north."

"I'm going to leave you now, Petey. You keep that bottle."

"You're sure a good friend. Old Petey will remember you."

Lyle rode back to the horse ranch and told Lafe what he had learned.

"I guess there ain't any way we're going to get anything more from that banker, Lafe."

"No, and it's kind of dangerous hangin' around. Somebody's going to get the idea to check this place out one of these days. Might be best if we take that thousand dollars we got out of this deal and head for New Mexico. That's a new area for us."

"What about that five hundred Artie offered if we finish off that Owens fellow, Lafe?"

"Mighty risky, Lyle. We can't lay for him in town and there's too many people around out at that ranch. Everybody's got our description, most likely."

"I guess you're right. We'll saddle up and head out in the morning."

On Saturday morning, Jed and Stan rode into town and stopped first at the Marshal's office. When Jed stepped inside, the Marshal met him with a smile.

"I have to thank you, Owens for suggesting that Mr Sinclair get me to go with him to the bank. That sure did me good to see that Amos Mason when that lawyer passed over the money and that mortgage release for Amos to sign. I thought Mason was going to faint away. Now why do you suppose that would affect him that way? It was just bank business and him just the manager, at least that's what he told everyone when he was getting old heck from people for stopping those cattle from being sold."

"I think Mason figured on getting his hands on that property himself. I don't know how much deviltry he might have been up to this past week but for sure, he was paying that station agent to keep him informed. I expect he had a tie in with what happened to me at the station the other night but I guess we'll never know."

"I've been askin' around and I found out that Mason visited Artie Smith a couple of times. I expect Artie's been wanting to get even with you and maybe he helped Mason set up that caper at the station. Nobody's seen those Bartons around so I guess they must have skipped out and good riddance."

"Could you tell me, Marshal, if there's a cattle buyer around. We need to get rid of some stock out there in the next week."

"Saw a man just yesterday having lunch just down the street here. Check with Betty, the waitress. She might be able to tell you something."

They stopped in at the Cafe and Jed asked the waitress if she was the one called Betty.

"I sure am."

"The Marshal told me he saw a man in here yesterday at lunch time. He thought he might be a cattle buyer. He said you maybe could give me something more."

"Al Scott. Sure he was here yesterday when the Marshal was here. I heard him ask someone if they knew of any cattle for sale. Said he'd be at the Windsor till tomorrow if they heard of any."

"Thanks, Betty. How about giving us some coffee and pie."

When they arrived at the Windsor Hotel, Lennie was behind the desk.

"Hello, Lennie. Hope your head feels better."

"Oh, sure, Mr Owens. What can I do for you? You're not here for a room are you. I heard you got that mortgage all straightened out and you boys were back to work."

"Right now we're looking for a cattle buyer and we've traced one here to your hotel, a man by the name of Al Scott."

"Sure, I know who you mean. Been here a couple of days but he's out right now. I saw him go by maybe twenty minutes ago. You could leave a message."

"Just tell him the Pritchard ranch has cattle for sale and they could be ready to ship in seven days."

"Sure, Mr Owens. I'll see that he gets the message."

When they came out of the hotel, Stan asked if they had anything left to do.

"I sure would like to send a message to Cheyenne but it ain't likely there will be anyone in Cheyenne to receive it. Maybe I'll write something later and send it in to be posted. Can't put much in a telegram anyways. Let's get back and help the boys get some work done. Sure wish I could have talked with that cattle buyer."

"Yeah, probably won't have long to wait for one to show. It's not too busy right now. You figure your trouble might be all over, Jed?"

"Some part of it is, for sure. Miss Ellen is safe enough now. She should be able to come to town whenever she wants. I've still got some enemies and so have you, those two guys you clobbered in the alley that night. There's a good chance they've seen you travelling with me and put two and two together, or one and one in this case. For me, it might be worse. That Artie Smith might have put a price on my head. I expect he's really stewing in his own juice right now, laying in bed with nothing to do but brood."

"You figure he's got that kind of money to pay out?"

"Didn't one of those boys mention five hundred if they left me in the alley that night? That five hundred most likely was offered by Artie Smith but if those boys are smart, they've already left. The Marshal said they weren't from around here and I can't see them hanging around waiting to be arrested."

When they got back to the ranch, they were just in time for the dinner gong.

There were somber faces when he said he hadn't found a buyer but they brightened again when he said he left word for one and he expected someone to show up, maybe as early as the afternoon.

Chapter 12

Artie Smith was back to his old whiny self now that he hadn't any more schemes to work on.

"How much longer, Doc?"

"If I had some way to get you moved, I'd send you home today."

"It won't be a day too soon for me, not that you haven't used me good, Doc but that place of mine is going down hill every day I'm away. Most likely there ain't much left now."

"Do you think you could travel if I was to get you a nice smooth wagon ride?"

"You give me enough of that pain killer, Doc and I'll make it."

"You can have some to take home with you but don't take more than I've been giving you here. It's not good to take too much for too long."

Later that afternoon, the Doctor visited Evans Funeral Parlour.

"Good afternoon, Doc. Got another one for me?"

"I've got a live one for you, Ed. Artie Smith. Could you haul him home tomorrow morning?"

"Yes, I could do that."

"Bring your slab to strap him onto and some men to load him. Sure will be good to get him out of the house."

"He got anyone out at his place, Doc? I heard those two

boys he had with him took off with loaded pack horses."

"He had an old Mexican cook there. I expect he's still around if there's any food left. Anyway, he has to go. He's driving my wife crazy."

"Okay, I'll get the boys together and transport him out and unload him. After that, he's on his own. He ever going to recover, Doc. That arm I mean?"

"There might be some things he'll be able to do with that hand but the shoulder will be stiff the rest of his life. Mean as that man is, it's a wonder he didn't give himself blood poison."

Ed smiled at Doc's surliness. "See you in the morning, Doc."

Meanwhile, Artie was scheming how he could get back at Owens now that he was staying around the area and had bought a half interest from Miss Ellen. Dammit, he would have done that. She had turned him down and took up with this stranger. Maybe he'd fix her bacon, too before it was over.

But it wouldn't be anyways soon, that's for sure. He had to recover and get as much use back in his right arm as he could. One thing he had asked the doctor was whether he could shoot from his right shoulder and the answer was a definite no. The recoil, Doc explained would cause enough pain that he would drop the gun and it could break the shoulder joint again. Whatever else happened, he wasn't going through this again.

When the doctor came back, he told Artie he'd made arrangements to have him moved home tomorrow morning and Artie accepted that to the doctor's surprise.

"You going downtown again this afternoon, Doc?"

"Not likely, Artie."

"Could you maybe hire a kid to take a note to Mel at the gun shop?"

"What on earth for, Artie? You can't fire a gun and you already have a gun here in this drawer."

"It's just not any gun that I'm wanting and I expect it will take some time to get it here. Just write a little note and tell Mel I need a new gun and would he drop by after he closes the shop."

"I guess I could do that, Artie but I hope this is not a scheme to get you in more trouble."

"I need a gun that a one armed man can use, Doc and I haven't got one. It's that simple."

After supper, Mel from the gun shop stopped by.

"How are you doin', Artie?"

"I'm movin' home tomorrow and I need to get me a long gun that a one armed man can handle and shoot off a gun rest. You got one or can you get me one, Mel?"

"Sure, Artie. The best thing is them newest Winchesters ... twenty-six in barrel, smokeless powder, thirty calibre, hold plenty of rounds. Might take a bit of practise to operate the action with one hand but lever action is just the same, right or left handed. I've got one down at the store right now."

"You bring that around here tomorrow morning, early and I'll pay for it. And bring me five boxes of ammunition."

"What would you like for sights, Artie? You going to be shooting long or short distance? I got three different sights."

"How about them ladder sights, Mel, like they had on them old Sharps."

"Sure I can put one on there for you, Artie. It'll take some shooting to find your ranges though."

"That's alright, Mel. It'll take some practise to shoot from the left shoulder and one handed, too."

"Okay. I'll fetch it around in the morning. First thing."

The next morning the gun was delivered and Artie was admiring it when Ed Evans showed up with the hearse.

"What are you doing here, Ed? You don't usually pick up live ones."

"First time, Artie. You need to be moved real careful like so we're going to carry you out on this slab and strap you down just like if you was dead."

"Just as long as you get me home without bustin' this shoulder loose again."

"We got the smoothest coach in town, Artie. So let's get you from that bed to this carrying slab. Got four of us here so we can take you out of here easy."

"You just hold up till Doc here gives me some of that pain killer."

So Artie was moved back to the horse ranch along with his new rifle and five boxes of ammunition.

Over the next month, all he could do was hold the gun and admire the action and the ladder sights that elevated to six hundred yards.

Finally, the day came when he took it outside, rested it across the porch rail and fired the first shot. There really wasn't much recoil and by holding the stock gripped up between his body and arm, he could lever a new shell into the firing chamber. The hard part was trying to aim while using his left eye. He decided that with practise and shooting from a rest, he could get good enough. At least he hoped so. But then again if he wound up dead, it wouldn't really matter. Half a man was no man at all.

Day after day, he practised and day after day he became more obsessed with the idea that he would make Jed Owens suffer at least as much as he was suffering and if he could get to shoot well enough, he would shoot him dead.

As more time wore on, his only thought was carrying out his mission. He forgot all about how he would get away with murder. That didn't matter anymore. Life didn't mean much anyway. He had spent what money he had and sold his horses. Now he was down to what land he owned and he'd take a loan on that if it was necessary. Just as long as the money held out till he had settled with Owens.

He had been riding out and checking the country. Two places were favorable for an ambush ... if he could catch Owens riding to town or if he could catch him riding within rifle range of that pile of rocks north of the ranch house.

The road to town presented the best chance. He could hide in some trees and make a getaway.

The pile of rocks, on the other hand presented a problem in getting away but it didn't deter him from checking it out. There were places a man could hide but he'd never be less than two hundred yards from the target because large boulders had over the years rolled down and out onto the range land. Any riders going out to the cattle or returning would naturally skirt around them but Artie felt that he had mastered the rifle range where he could make a killing shot up to three hundred yards with a rest to support the rifle.

The easiest way would be to sneak around the ranch at night but there was a dog that had already shown his dislike and if he was scented by the dog and sent running before he had accomplished his mission, everyone on the ranch would be alerted.

He figured that right now Owens felt pretty safe. Two months had gone by and no trouble had come to the Pritchard place. Owens had bought himself in for half interest and everything was going fine. Surely, pretty soon, Owens would start getting careless. Every time he'd seen him through the field glasses, he'd been riding with a stranger he heard had come down from Cheyenne with him.

For days he watched the road to town but Owens never showed. Twice he saw Miss Ellen with Old Rolly going for supplies. Owens seemed to be spending his time on the ranch.

He finally decided he had to check out that rock pile. He was quite sure he could find concealment but getting to it was a problem. He either had to ride to the back side and leave his horse tethered where there was no feed or water or he had to leave his horse in the regular place and walk along the foot of the ridge until he came to where the pile of rock protruded far enough out that he might get a shot.

If he moved over that rock pile in daylight, he could be easily seen so he had to be in position before it became light.

He spent two days selecting his place of concealment then with a coil of rope, he marked the best route from the top of the ridge. Now in darkness he could make his descent and be waiting for Owens to ride within range.

Unknown to Artie Smith, Jed was being kept up to date about Artie, his activities with the rifle and how much ammunition he bought. It was enough to put a damper on Jed's good feeling about how the ranch was shaping up.

Everyday he gave his orders to Rickey and Chad then he and Stan took a different area to work. There was no reason to have men he didn't know that well in danger. He knew that Stan understood they were in constant danger. Both rode with saddle guns loaded and a wary eye on the surroundings.

For some reason the dog, Tige always tagged along, sensing somehow that Jed was the boss and looking to take his orders from him.

This cool morning, the dog was trotting along behind the horses. He was always anxious to get to the cattle so Jed would give him some signal and he could get busy doing what he liked to do.

Over the last month, the dog had discovered that if he scooted up behind a horse and grabbed the hair just above the hoof, the horse would speed up. Sometimes the horse would kick but Tige was smart enough to duck then he would go to Stan's horse and do the same. The dog apparently felt that in doing this, they would reach the cattle sooner and he could get to work.

This morning, he was at his game. He scooted up to Jed's horse and nipped at his heels and sure enough the horse jumped ahead and at the same time, there was a rifle report from the left that set the dog running in circles not knowing what was going on. Meantime, Stan's horse took to bucking and switching ends like he had gotten himself into a hornets nest.

Jed knew instantly that they were under attack from someone on that rock pile and when he looked he saw some small movement about fifty feet up the hillside. He swung his horse straight towards the gunman. If he could reach the base of the hill, he could be out of sight of where the gunman was crouched.

Stan, in the meantime was getting the ride of his life. The bullet had grazed his horse across the rump and he was letting Stan know he didn't appreciate such harsh treatment. Horse and rider went in among the rocks that had fallen down the hillside over the years and Stan realized that if the horse threw him, he would likely land on something pretty hard. He slipped his saddle gun free, picked what he figured was an opportune time and leaped to the ground.

Jed reached the base of the hill with only one more shot being fired at him. He jumped from the saddle and took refuge behind a boulder. He had no way to advance on the gunman so he stayed down and looked to where Stan had jumped from the saddle. He realized Stan was doing the same as himself, just staying close to the ground and waiting to see what the gunman would do.

From up the hill, he heard Artie Smith bellow.

"Damn you, Owens. You're not getting away. I've been waiting too long for this. Now I'm coming to get you."

Then Artie came out of his cover and started down toward Jed. While he was doing this, Stan could see him plain as day and aimed a shot that knocked Artie off his feet and the rifle came scuttering down the rocks.

"I got him, Jed."

"Be careful of him, Stan. There's a lot of hate there. He

could rouse up and bite you yet."

"I got him through the left arm, I think so I don't see how he could be much threat if it's Artie Smith."

Meantime, Artie was barely conscious from the pain. The shot had busted his left arm and the right shoulder had broken loose where it was mended. Artie clenched his teeth against the pain and reminded himself that he had to kill Jed Owens.

He made that broken shoulder work enough that he drew his side gun which he wore butt forward on his right side and he waited with his mind closed down against the pain. He could hear the two men working their way up through the rocks but he didn't hear the padded feet of Tige as he made his way up above him. Tige was now not more than four feet away watching warily toward the man that he had now figured out was trying to hurt the boss. For now the man was lying quiet and didn't seem to present a danger but until Jed arrived and told him different, he'd just stay still and watch.

As Jed and Stan got within fifteen feet from Artie, he shoved his gun out under his left arm. That was the signal the dog was waiting for. He made his jump and clamped his jaws on Artie's wrist, the gun fired and the bullet went between Stan and Jed.

The strain was too much for Artie Smith to hold on any longer. He passed out.

"Doggone it, Jed. He was a fighter."

"Not a fighter, Stan. A madman. He's been planning this for months. That's all he's lived for. Now he's got his left arm shot up with a rifle bullet. If he don't bleed to death, he'll have to have it taken off most likely. You can see the pieces of bone."

"What are we going to do with him, Jed?"

"You stay with him. I'll go to town and report to the Marshal or the Sheriff, whoever I can find and I'll bring the Doc back with me if I can. Maybe he can truss him up so we can move him down that hill. I guess we're going to need a wagon, too."

"He ain't hardly worth losing a days work over. I doubt if he comes through this one."

"I didn't think he'd live the last time but here he is, trying to get me again."

"And maybe if he lives, Jed, he'll try again. Maybe we should just finish what we started and end it."

"Could you pull your gun and finish him off right now, Stan?"

"No, I don't think I could. I could do it for a horse or a cow but dammit, it ain't the same."

"Okay, you stay here. I'll send Miss Ellen out from the house with something for a bandage for that left arm and I guess we could give him a drink of whiskey if he wakes up. It might help kill the pain."

When Jed got back to the house, Miss Ellen was on the verandah.

"What happened, Jed. I heard shots? Where's Stan? Did he get hurt?"

"Stan's fine, Miss Ellen. Artie Smith tried to bushwack us and Stan wounded him. He's partway up that rock pile. Could you take something for a bandage and if there's some whiskey around, take that along. I have to ride to town, report it to the Marshal or the Sheriff and see if I can get the doctor."

"Why bother. That man has caused more trouble than he's worth. Leave him for the buzzards."

"Miss Ellen, that's what I thought at first but you and me, we're made different than he is. It would haunt us till we die. No, I've got to do what I can for him although I doubt if he lives through this. He busted his right shoulder when he fell but you can't do anything for that. The doctor will have to strap it up or something so we can get him down from there.

"Stan's with him but you be careful around him. He's more ornery than a bad horse. Both his arms are broken but he might try to kick you and he might even bite. He hates you most as much as he hates me and for a longer time."

"It's really going to make it hard to do anything for him, knowing how he hates us both."

"Just do what you can to keep him alive till the Doc gets here."

Jed left and hurried into town. He stopped at Doctor Fraser's house first. When he knocked, the doctor's wife answered the door.

"Is the Doctor home, Mrs Fraser?"

"No, he had an early call out of town to a birthing. Can't tell when he might be back."

"We have a man out at the ranch needs attention though it might not do any good. Artie Smith got himself shot again."

"God forgive me but I hope it's fatal. That man should never have survived that first gunshot. I swear the man only survived because he was hatching something up with the visitors he was having here. Kept me busy, it did just answering the door.

"One time while I was down at the store, someone came in the house by the back way and tramped mud right through my kitchen. I'm guessing it was one of the Barton twins. I didn't know about them and what they were up to at the time. Then there was the old drunk, Petey and even the bank manager, that Amos Mason who was trying to get that Pritchard woman's ranch."

"I see. Now, Mrs Fraser, you tell your husband I've been in. I have to report this to the Marshal or the Sheriff, if he's around this area."

"I sure hope my husband doesn't bring that man back here but I'll tell him when he gets back."

When Jed arrived at the Marshal's office, he was in luck. The Marshal was seated at his desk doing paper work and mumbling to himself.

"I've got something more interesting than that paper work for you, Herb. You've been telling me for two months now about how Artie Smith's been planning something. This morning, he tried for me out at the ranch."

"Did you shoot him dead this time?"

"No, I didn't shoot him at all but Stan winged him pretty bad. He probably won't make it, he's in sort of a bad place to get him out of. He's up in that rock pile north of the ranch house. I stopped by Doc Fraser's house but he's out and his wife says there's no telling when he might get back. Artie busted that shoulder loose again when he fell in them rocks so I don't know how we're going to get him out of there. I was hoping you or the Sheriff might come out and look things over in case this comes to an inquest."

"The Sheriff ain't in town. I know that for a fact so I'll ride out with you and I might get Ed Evans up at the funeral home to go out with his hearse. He has a stretcher and straps. Maybe we could bring him down on that. Artie's already had one trip in that hearse. Ed took him home from Doc Fraser's place two months ago. How many times can he ride that thing before we can say a final good-bye to him. First, I need to get my horse and then see Ed so you go on back. I won't be long."

When Jed got back to the rock pile, everything looked the same. Miss Ellen had put a tourniquet on Artie's left arm and bandaged it. Artie seemed to be out cold.

"How is he, Stan?"

"Unconscious right now, Jed. Thank God for that. He was awake when Miss Ellen came and the language he used wasn't fit for a muleskinner's ears. I felt like hitting him over the head. I told Miss Ellen to just forget him and go back to the house but she refused. He passed out while we were fixing that tourniquet and he hasn't come to since."

"The doctor's out of town to a birthing, his wife says and there's no tellin' how long he'll be. The Marshal says the undertaker has the best equipment to get him down from here and he was going to see if he could locate him. I'm kind of curious, Stan about how Artie got over that rock pile. He must have a horse on the other side. Would you go check and turn the horse loose. He'll go back to Artie's."

When Stan got up to where Artie had fired the first shot, he hollered to Jed and held up a rope so Jed could see that it came right down the face of the hill.

So that was how Artie found his way down here to his hiding place before daylight. It was hard to believe what a man would go through for revenge.

When the Marshal arrived, Jed showed him how the shooting had taken place and how Artie had found his way down through that rock pile in the dark.

"If it hadn't been for the dog nipping at my horses heels, Artie probably would have got me. The dog saved me again when Artie attempted to shoot me with his six gun."

"I guess that dog proved who man's best friend is this morning, Jed. Well, I see Ed coming. It would be best if Artie stayed unconscious till Ed gets him down off the rock pile. Where's Stan, Jed? We're going to need four men to move that stretcher of Ed's."

"I sent him over the hill to turn Artie's horse loose. It will wander on back to the ranch. Do you know if there's anyone there to take the gear off when it gets there?"

"That old Mexican has been into town regular, buyin' supplies and ammunition for Artie. I guess he's still there. I'll send Gary out to check and tell the old guy Artie won't be around for awhile, if ever. Let's get that stretcher up here and get Artie on it before he comes to."

They were all trying to work out how they were going to protect all of Artie's injured parts when the Marshal came up with a solution.

"Let me put the cuffs on him. We'll just lay his hands

across his body and I'll cuff him up short then we'll put one of these straps beneath his shoulders. Ed, you take his feet. Jed and I will take this strap and Stan, you get his head. Then we'll lift him right onto that stretcher. Then it's just a matter of getting through those rocks without dumping him off."

It took some manoeuvring but they finally got Artie loaded into the hearse.

The Marshal turned to Jed.

"There's no need for you boys to come into town today. I'll make out a report and wait till the Sheriff comes by and give it to him. He might want to talk to you. He's not quite up on what's been going on around here. He has the whole county to patrol."

"We'll wait and see if Artie pulls through this time."

"Doc Fraser's Missus sure ain't going to be happy, seeing him come back."

"I don't know how they'll make out with him this time unless they can find someone to help. Anyway, we've done our duty by him and thank God he stayed unconscious while we carried him off that rock pile."

Chapter 13

Jed, Stan and Miss Ellen had little to say as they rode back to the ranch house.

Jed and Stan went directly to the stable and doctored up the bullet wound on Stan's horse.

Miss Ellen went to the house and brewed up some coffee and set the bottle of whiskey on the table. Maybe the boys would like to put a bit in their coffee.

Rolly came into the stable before Jed and Stan finished with the horse.

"Did you boys finish him off this time?"

"No, Rolly. He was still alive when they left for town with him. He's just living on spite it seems."

"You should've just put another slug in him where it would do the most good, Jed. If he lives, he'll be back."

"I don't know how he could hurt us now, Rolly unless he gets the rabies and bites us. The Marshal tells me he hasn't any money left and his ranch is mortgaged. By the time he's healed up, most likely the bank will have foreclosed. There's no way he'll ever get money enough to hire anyone to do anything for him. No, I think we've seen the last of Artie Smith. Let's head for the house. Miss Ellen said she'd have coffee ready."

Hot coffee, warmed up biscuits and bacon were on the table when they arrived. Miss Ellen brought the coffee pot and poured each of them a mug and one for herself.

"I didn't need to give Artie Smith any of that whiskey but I thought I'd leave it out for you men. It might settle your nerves down some."

Rolly reached for the bottle.

"Well, Miss Ellen, I haven't been out of the yard all mornin' but my nerves have been actin' up something awful ever since I heard that first shot. What happened out there, Jed. I heard four shots, near as I can remember."

"Artie Smith was hunkered down in that rock pile. Lord knows how many times he's waited there. Stan and I were just riding along. This morning we rode pretty close to those rocks. You know how the dog likes to hurry the horses on a cool morning like this? Well, just as Artie was pulling the trigger, Tige nipped my horse's heels. The horse spurted ahead and the shot went behind me and ripped a groove in the rump of Stan's horse. You should have seen Stan ride that devil.

"Anyway, Stan managed to get off the horse with his saddle gun, out of sight over to Artie's left. Artie paid no attention to him. He had eyes only for me. I put the spurs to my horse and rode straight for that rock pile. I drew one more shot but I don't know where it went.

"When I got to the rock pile, Artie couldn't see me and he was so full of rage, he left his hiding place and started down the slope towards me in full view of Stan. Stan fired one round and ruined Artie's left elbow. When Artie fell, it seems he busted that right shoulder again.

"Stan and I started up the slope towards where Artie lay but you know, that man was so full of hate, he managed somehow to get his side arm out with his right hand and then he laid there playin' dead.

"When Stan and I were almost to him, he poked the gun out to fire but Tige was just above him, watching. You know how he can do that. Well, that dog jumped and grabbed

Artie's hand. Artie managed to pull the trigger but he missed Stan and myself. That reminds me, I've got to treat that dog like a long lost brother from now on."

"By God, Jed. What a yarn! Sure wish I could get to town and sidle up to the bar. That sure would be worth a drink or two."

"Didn't I hear Miss Ellen say she needed some things? Why don't you harness up and drive her in. You're needing to go aren't you, Miss Ellen?"

"I've hardly got time now. There's things I need to do for supper."

"You go right along. Stan and I can throw something together for the boys. This afternoon, we'll lay out the plans for that cookhouse we've been talkin' about. Meantime, if you hear tell of a cook needing a job, hire him on. He can help with the construction."

After Rolly and Miss Ellen left for town, Jed and Stan went out in the yard and eyed up just where the cookhouse should be.

"I have a notion, Stan that we should build a cookhouse and a new bunkhouse like we had on the *Rocking O* with a breezeway and all. What do you think?"

"I like the idea. What are you going to use for material?"

"I've been lookin' along the slope on our north boundary and there's plenty of timber. We could build it of logs. We got the time with these mild Texas winters and the boys are having trouble keeping busy. That's why I haven't been riding out with them lately. If I were along, they'd feel guilty with nothing much to do."

"Speaking of that, Jed, what are we going to do between now and time to cook supper?"

"Let's go check that timber out and figure out the easiest way to get it here. Some of it might be two or three miles away. You got any ideas?"

"No, I don't. Up north we'd most likely bring them in on a sled this time of year."

"Now you've got me wondering how John's making out. I'm sure he didn't get ready for winter the way he should have. He didn't have the manpower to get what hay he should have had, I know that."

"The boys wouldn't work for John the way they would for you or Ben. John just didn't get the same loyalty."

"I'm going to try and get up there next spring and find out how things are. I wrote a couple of letters but I haven't heard anything back. I expected Rose to keep me posted."

All afternoon, Jed and Stan rode. They checked every stand of timber that Jed figured belonged on the Pritchard land. Some he wasn't too certain of. He'd have to check the land map back at the house and run some markers somehow or bring in a surveyor. That might be best.

If what he was seeing today was any indication, there was valuable timber that could be harvested during slack times, like right now. He never liked to lay men off in slack times, especially good hands. They might hire on somewhere else and the men he had were loyal to Miss Ellen. He hoped by now they had accepted him as their foreman.

One reason he needed the cook house was that he thought Miss Ellen could use a break. She had been under a terrible strain till that mortgage had been settled and now she had to cook every day for the men.

Also, there was the matter of his feelings for Miss Ellen. He had held back, making no move and saying nothing because he knew that things hadn't been settled with Artie Smith. He realized he might have been killed this morning and if he had declared his intentions, where would that have left Miss Ellen, providing of course, she had allowed him to call on her at the house. Now, surely Artie couldn't cause any more trouble.

"You've been quiet, Jed. Even more that usual. You never was one to talk a man's head off. What have you got on your mind?"

"You ever think about getting married, Stan?   Settling down?"

"So that's what's got you so quiet. The boys have been wonderin' why you and Miss Ellen don't make it a full partnership. Is that why you all of a sudden decided we needed a new cookhouse right today. And you've been holding back till after Artie made his move. Is that right?"

"That's right, Stan. I knew from what the Marshal told me, Artie was up to something and there was no sense making plans till after that was past. I'm thanking you for being there this morning."

"I surely was in the right place. That danged horse bucked me right into the right spot and then Artie kind of went wild. I realized he'd missed his chance, left his cover and started right towards you, never paying a bit of attention to me."

"Well, let's get back, Stan and see if we can find something to cook for supper."

"We'll find something, Jed then we'll feed them the story about what happened this morning. There ain't a one of them will leave the table figuring they should get more."

Supper was over and everything cleaned up before Rolly and Miss Ellen came back from town.

"I hope you had supper in town, Miss Ellen. The boys cleaned out everything Stan and I cooked up."

"Yes, we did. We stopped at Sally's. I think Rolly wanted to get a few cups of strong coffee before he arrived back. When he said that story would be worth a few drinks, he meant about a dozen. I drove the buggy as far as Sally's and Rolly sang the whole way. But don't say anything. Rolly's been about as strung out as I have been, sitting around here waiting for who knew what to happen. I heard in town that

Artie's still alive and as crazy as a hoot owl. When he woke up and realized he had failed, he just broke. Went completely insane so Doctor Fraser told some of the men."

"I guess we'd have done a kindness if we'd let him die this morning."

"It ain't likely he'll live long anyway. The doctor says he won't be still. As soon as the pain killer wears off and he wakes, he goes right back to thrashing and raving till the pain puts him unconscious again."

"That's enough about Artie, Miss Ellen. Stan and I made a few decisions while you were gone. Made plans for a new bunkhouse and cookhouse all under one roof with a breezeway between. What do you think?"

"I think that's wonderful and we can keep everyone busy all winter long."

"I'm sure there's lots of timber so we can build it out of logs but I need to locate the boundaries. Do you have a map of your grant?"

"I'm sure there's one here but it will only show the corners. I think you'll have to figure out where you are along the side lines. Father said before he died, he would have to get a survey done."

"Okay. As long as we can find the northeast and the northwest corners, we can run a line pretty close so we can get enough timber for the cookhouse. In the meantime, we'll try to get a land surveyor to do all the side lines. I've got a plan that will keep us with a full crew for years to come."

"I've got a letter here from your sister, Rose. Maybe you should read it before you go to the bunkhouse. There's better light in here."

"How come she addressed it to you?"

"Maybe she was afraid you might not get it if she addressed it to you. She doesn't know how notorious you are down here."

Jed took the letter and started reading.

"She says they've already had some pretty cold weather up there and enough snow that Del made a sled to use for when he had to go to town. She says everything's well with them and Papa but she doesn't know how John is making out on the *Rocking O*.

"Jack Benson is staying for the winter. That's Mother's youngest brother. I just met him in Cheyenne before we left. Papa and Del needed help so Papa hired him on for what he said would be a month. I guess things must have worked out. Rose says I wouldn't believe what Jacks' big dog can do. Wouldn't she be surprised that your dog saved my life twice this morning, although the first time wasn't planned."

"Jed, Sally told me they are having a party at the school house in Breckenridge on Saturday. They have a get together a couple of times a year. I didn't go at all for the last year. First it was Father dying, then the problems with Artie Smith. Sally thought since you and I are partners here that we should both come and you could meet the neighbors. What do you think? Are you interested? I know you have a lot to think about."

"Sure, Miss Ellen. I'd be glad to go but I'll have to go to Richardson and get some new clothes. I don't have anything fittin' to escort a lady to any sort of social."

"We'll be having supper there so I'll leave something here for the boys to warm. It sure will be nice to get out around again."

"I best be gettin' down to the bunkhouse, Miss Ellen. I'm kind of looking forward to Saturday."

"Stop in before you go to town. I might need some little thing. It's going to be pot luck for the supper. Each woman will bring something."

After Jed left, Ellen sat down and read the special note Rose had sent to her.

TEXAS BOUND   Arnold McKay

Dear Miss Ellen,

First off, excuse me for being forward but I have to tell you about Jed. He's the most considerate man I know, especially where a woman is concerned. I'm going by how he was with Mama and myself. For quite awhile, he was the only friend I had, except of course my husband, Del.

If Jed is a bit stiff and constrained toward you, Miss Ellen, he's probably scared that he'll make a mistake and offend. You may have to do a few unladylike things like maybe do a little bit of scheming. But if I know Jed, as soon as he gets the notion you might be interested in him, he'll come around mighty quick. I'm sure you know by now that Jed doesn't waste any time once he's set his mind so get ready for a wedding.

I hope I haven't over-stepped myself but I so love that brother of mine, I just can't let him make a mistake. So if you have any feelings for Jed, go get him. If you don't, let him down easy.

Respectfully,
Rose Ramsey

Good Lord, what a woman she must be. Already her advice had paid off. Sure Sally had told her about the party at the old school house but anyone who showed up with a man would be considered a couple and this would be the first time Miss Ellen would be showing up with a man. And what a man!

As for Jed, he made his way to the bunkhouse, whistling a tune he'd never known was in his head. He'd stayed behind after the boys left to read that letter and he had some idea he might start to speak to Miss Ellen about the future and by gosh he'd get it done.

They were stepping out together on Saturday and

somewhere between here and town, he'd let Miss Ellen know how he felt.

When Saturday rolled around, Jed hooked up the buckboard and drove over to the house. When Miss Ellen stepped through the door, he was flabbergasted. She was downright beautiful. How could such a woman have any interest in him.

He was so nervous, he almost let her fall as he helped her into the buckboard. By some miracle when she fell back, he caught her and she turned and faced him with a smile.

"Now, Jed Owens, you surely wouldn't let a lady fall down in the dust would you?"

"Miss Ellen, I'd lay down and let you fall on top of me. I surely would."

"Well, let's give it another try, shall we. I'm not used to climbing up on this thing with a dress on."

When they got started for town, Miss Ellen moved across the seat so she was touching Jed and danged if he could remember which rein was which. The horse must have been more confused that he was.

At the party, folks came up to them and talked away, like he and Miss Ellen were married or something. Not that he would mind but it must be embarrassing for Miss Ellen.

On their way home, Jed had to say something about how sorry he was about the way people acted.

"It didn't embarrass me, Jed unless it embarrassed you."

"No, Miss Ellen. It made me right proud."

"Then we're agreed, we make a fine couple."

"Miss Ellen, I been thinkin' for some time now but this thing with Artie Smith, it's been hangin' over us so I ain't said nothin' and maybe I shouldn't now but you and me, we sort of fit together don't we?"

"What is it you'd like to say, Jed?"

"I reckon I'm sayin' we ought to get married and make this partnership a full partnership. That's what I'm saying."

"I surely would admire to be your wife, Jed. The way those folks took to you tonight told me for sure what I already knew. You're a fine man, Jed Owens and I'll be proud to be your wife."

"Miss Ellen, I can hardly believe it."

At this opportune time, the horse felt an urge to relieve itself and Miss Ellen turned to Jed and put her arms around his neck.

"Hold me, Jed and stop calling me Miss Ellen. Call me Ellie. That's what father called me and he always said that he loved me from the time I was a little girl."

"Okay, Miss Ellen, I mean Ellie but what will the boys think?"

"Most likely, what took you so long, especially Rolly. I could see him watching and shaking his head for a month now."

When they got to the ranch, Jed stopped the buggy by the verandah steps and walked around to help Ellie down. When he did, she hung on and turned her face up to be kissed and because Jed hesitated, Ellie pulled his head down and kissed him a long time. Finally, she let him go."

"Miss Ellie, I don't know what to say."

"Didn't you like kissing me, Jed."

"I surely did, Miss Ellie but I don't want to seem improper bold."

"I think you've already done that, Jed. You proposed marriage on our first date."

Then she laughed.

"Good night, Jed. Don't forget to put the horse away."

"Sure, Miss Ellie, sure. I'll do that. Good night, Miss Ellie."

When Ellen got through the door, she put her hands together, looked towards the ceiling and said "*Thank you, sister Rose*".

For the next month, Jed was somewhere on cloud nine. It

was a good thing the boys could work on their own. In fact, if they wanted any work out of Jed, they had to tell him what to do.

Rolly found a cook in town and then they had to purchase a whole new kitchen outfit, starting with a new stove.

When the cook room was ready, Jed told the men they would have to use the old bunkhouse for another week. Before they put anything in the new building, other than a stove, they would have a wedding party. Each man was told to bring a girl if he had one or if he knew one well enough, to ask her to come.

Miss Ellie was making her list of friends and it didn't seem that long so she put a notice in Sally's Cafe announcing the marriage and get together at the ranch.

As it turned out, the house was full, the bunkhouse was full and the ladies were put to work in the new cookhouse to cook up extra food though some had brought food with them.

After the party ran down and everyone went home, Jed dug out some extra whiskey and set it out for the ranch hands.

"It seems you fellows have been holding back a might. Maybe you didn't want to do anything to embarrass Miss Ellen and me. We're leaving for town now so you have yourself a time and tomorrow's a holiday."

"Dammit, Jed, you're the best, you and Miss Ellen both. Get along with you now so we can get started."

When Jed and Ellen got back to the ranch, everything had been moved from the old bunkhouse to the new and Jed's belongings were dumped either just inside the door or on the verandah.

Ricky met them at the verandah steps.

"You and the Missus go right on in. We'll look after the rig and you're invited to take your next meal in the new cookhouse."

"Thanks, Ricky and thank the boys for me for helping out

so much yesterday. I had better get inside and try to find room for my stuff."

Chapter 14

The winter flew by. Jed hired a surveyor to put up cairns
between the corners so they would know where the side lines
were. Then he told the crew what his plan was.

"All that timber inside those side lines should be thinned
out. My idea is to get a contract for railroad ties then we can
work right along all winter and no one need be laid off. In
fact, next spring if we find the right man, we'll hire him."

"Jed, you're a marvel. It's hard if you're laid off for three
or four months. You wind up with your money gone and ridin'
the grub line."

"Maybe we should keep this quiet till I get a contract and
I'll try to get the contract for more than one year. There's more
than one ranch around here with timber on it."

The rest of the winter went quickly and soon Ellen was
asking when they could go north.

"I'm dying to meet your family, Jed. When can we go."

"Let's say we go in two weeks and you better be prepared
to sleep in the barn. I know Rose and Del have no room and
Papa just has a little cabin with a double bunk for himself and
Jack."

"We'll be all right, Jed. I just can't wait any longer."

Two weeks later, they were on their way. They hit a snow
storm in Kansas that threatened to block the tracks but after
that the sun came out. The train travelled slow and the

engineers watched for washouts from the runoff.

Finally, they reached Cheyenne and Jed said they should stop by the livery and tell Charlie they needed transportation the next day.

"By golly, Jed, you came back! Ben said you might come up this spring and this must be Mrs Owens since you seem to be together."

"Yes, Charlie. This is Ellen Pritchard, or she used to be. Now she's an Owens."

"I'm glad to know you, Ellen. I knew there was something down there in Texas had Jed's attention. When he brought those bulls back last fall, he was sure trampin' at the bit to get aboard that train. I swear he might of give those bulls away if I hadn't stepped in and got him some good deals."

"Say Charlie, you still have that fancy carriage folks like to take for Sunday drives?"

"I sure do. It ain't been used much yet this year though I suppose the young men will start lining up to rent it soon."

"Could we have it for a week, Charlie?"

"You sure can, Jed. I hope you can get over that road to your Pa's place. We surely did have a hum-dinger of a winter. I don't know what's left of the *Rocking O*. We had one heck of a freeze. We had two feet of snow then a thaw that melted down to about four inches then it turned cold. Ice froze right to everything. The stock couldn't dig for feed and they couldn't move very far because it was so dang slippery. Every rancher had losses but from what I heard, your brother was the worst hit."

"Well, we'll see you in the morning, Charlie. We have to get a bit of supper and a room for the night. You mind if I leave some of this baggage here?"

"No problem, Jed. You'll find that fancy carriage right at the back. Just put your stuff in there and you'll be half loaded come mornin'. Sure glad to meet you, Miss Ellen."

"Nice to meet you, too. Bye, Charlie."

"Let's stop by Mae's Cafe and have supper. It's not as fancy as the hotel dining room but the food is better."

As they seated themselves at a table, Mae came through from the kitchen.

"Jed Owens, my lands, where did you drop from and this must be the reason you was in such a hurry to get back to Texas last fall."

"Mae, this is Ellie. Ellie Owens, she is now."

"I have to say, Miss Ellie, you captured a good one but how you managed it, I'll never know. This boy was about as shy around women folks as a three legged wolf around a steel trap."

"Bring us some coffee, Mae then dish us up some grub. The train ran late and we haven't eaten for hours."

When they were booked into their hotel room and had their boots off, Ellen turned to Jed.

"It sure makes a girl proud when she sees folks who knew her husband all their life greet him the way they greeted you, Jed."

"I saw some admirers that weren't lookin' my way when we walked down the street. I could see it in their eyes, especially old Charlie. He's likely bellied up to the bar describing you down to the last curl on your head."

"I just hope I measure up for your Pa."

"Don't you worry none about that. Papa will be so pleased to see you, he might squeeze you in two."

"Well, he's going to just have to hold himself in check. There's more than one of me here to squeeze and that other one is sort of fragile."

"Ellie, what are you sayin'? Are you and me, are we gonna have us a young'un?"

"We surely are, Jed. That's why I've been so anxious to make this trip before I get too big. When a woman gets big in the middle, she sure don't feel too attractive."

"You'll still look beautiful to me, Ellie and it will surely please Papa. He loves Rose's young'uns but he'll be real happy to have a grandchild with the Owens name."

"I'm pretty tired, Jed. Let's get some rest. I take it we'll have a long trip tomorrow?"

"If the roads are as bad as Charlie thinks they might be, then it could be after dark before we get there. I'm glad we brought some blankets along. It's going to be cold in the mornin' riding in that buggy and we'll need them out at Rose's, most likely. I can't see them havin' much extra."

In the morning, Jed asked the cook to make some sandwiches for them. At the livery, Charlie had put in some oats for the horses.

"I guess you won't have any trouble gettin' water for the horses. We've had too dang much this spring. You tell Del to bring whatever corn and oats he has left as soon as it dries out a bit and say hello for me to the rest of the folks."

As soon as they left Cheyenne behind, Jed was glad they had taken the carriage that was pulled by two horses and they were two of Charlie's best. The going was so hard that one horse would never last the day pulling a rig. It would be late beans before they reached Rose's place.

It was near the end of April. The sun was getting high in the sky and it warmed up nicely by midday but the ground was saturated so that it didn't dry much.

"Do we go by the *Rocking O*, Jed?"

"No, we cut across. It's a bit shorter. Would you like to see the place?"

"Not today. I guess if it's shorter to go straight there, that's the way we'd better go. What do you think took place at the ranch this winter? Charlie at the livery said the *Rocking O* got hit the worst."

"John didn't get along well with the men and I expect he was short of hay for winter feed. Some years, you don't need any extra but other times, and I guess this past winter was one, we would need at least enough for two weeks.

"You can ration it out, mind you but if cattle don't get something to eat and digest, their body heat drops down till they just give up. I don't expect you ever get that problem in Texas."

"No, we don't get that problem. Occasionally, there's a blizzard down that far south and I think we should think about putting up hay and keepin' our stock count down. Ship everything in the fall that we can possibly ship."

"I sure do like the way you can grasp this ranchin' business, Ellie. Makes it a lot easier for me to think out loud."

"I can't get over how things turned around when you came along down there. My father did okay when he was alive and if he had lived we would not have gotten into those problems. But you stepped in and the boys didn't resent you. They just assumed you would do what was needed."

"Twenty thousand dollars from Papa didn't hurt either."

"That's true. We could never have done it without that money. Let's never mortgage the place again."

"I'm all for that. When you're in the ranching business, you never know when you might get a bad year. If my idea about ties for the railroad works out, we should be able to put money aside for a bad year."

"How much farther, Jed?"

"I'd say we might get there in time to unhitch in daylight. The days are gettin' a lot longer this far north. You think this is tough country for cattle but there's ranches well up into Canada. The days are really lengthening up there I expect."

"I can see a building, Jed. Is that where we're going?"

"It surely is and we're going to make it before these nags play out."

When they pulled into the yard, they were met by the biggest, ugliest looking dog Jed had ever seen.

"I'm not getting down from here before someone calls that dog back, Jed."

The door opened and Ruthie ran out.

"Uncle Jed, Uncle Jed! Come here, Rufe and let Uncle Jed down. Who's with you, Uncle Jed?"

The dog walked back, circled around Ruthie and sat by her side.

"Ruthie, this is Ellie. She's my wife and she might let you call her your Aunt Ellie since you don't have any other Aunts."

"You can get down Aunt Ellie. Rufe won't hurt you, not unless I get scared or somethin'."

"What's going on out there, Ruthie? Who are you talkin' to?"

"It's Uncle Jed and Aunt Ellie, Mama. Uncle Jed's a feared of Rufe."

"Good Lord, Jed. Get down and bring your new bride in here where we can see her. Ruthie, you send that dog to the barn. He's so big, he gets in the way."

Del came out and he and Jed shook hands and Del took a good look at Ellie.

"I told you, Rose, that brother of yours always could pick the best horse in the corral."

"Go on with you, Del. Go fetch Papa."

"He must be nappin' or he'd of heard the ruckus."

"Miss Ellen, I'm so glad you're here so we can finally meet face to face. I got your note about the wedding and then nothing since."

"Jed told me there was no use in writing, you probably wouldn't get the letter anyway. I couldn't believe what he was sayin' till we started here today."

"Well, wait till Papa gets here and sees you and Jed. Then we women folks will go to the kitchen and have some woman talk.

Jed and Del went to find Ben and the women went toward the kitchen.

We'll make up something for you and Jed to eat. You must be half starved."

"I guess we must be sort of hungry but we will survive. My heaven, Rose, that Ruthie is ordering that big dog around."

"That dog adores her. Sometimes she just whispers in his ear what she wants and he obeys. It's not our dog. It came here with Uncle Jack though he says it really doesn't belong to him. I'm afraid Jack might leave someday and that dog will go with him. It sure would be a sad day for Ruthie though I keep telling her it's Jack's dog. What's the big news with you and Jed, Miss Ellen? Did something special make you rush your trip up here?"

"I'm going to have a baby, Rose and I wanted you to know almost before Jed. I just told him last night."

"I just knew it. I can tell a happy pregnant woman every time."

"I'm so grateful to you, Rose for sending me that note in with that letter to Jed. He never knew he was being set up by his own sister! You were right. As soon as he got the notion I might be partial to marriage, it was full steam ahead. Married seven weeks after our first date which I started arranging the same day I got your note. I'm sure he would have gotten around to it eventually anyway.

"There was trouble and you know Jed, he wanted to keep me out of it as much as he could. That's all behind us now and things are fine at home. How are you folks doing? We heard in town that this area had a hard winter."

"We're fine. I expect Jed has told you about what Del is doin' here with the pigs, the hens, the grain and garden and such and now we have a few head of cattle. We survived quite well. Come, let's have a peek in at little Stan. He's sleeping."

"You mean you named him after the same Stan Murphy

184

who came down with Jed?"

"Oh, yes. Jed suggested it. Stan and Del worked together a lot before Del and I got married and Del liked Stan so we gave him that name."

"I suppose I'll have to start lookin' for a name for our baby soon."

"Just don't name it Jed. Not the first boy at least. Papa won't cotton to that at all."

"Why, Rose?"

"He just figures every baby should have it's own name. If Stan had been living here, he would've raised a fuss about my boy's name. Here he is, Miss Ellen, sleeping like a baby should. He is really good, no trouble at all but I'm sure before he's a man, he will give us lots of worries."

"He's adorable, Rose. I can hardly wait till tomorrow to see him awake."

"Let's get that coffee on, Miss Ellen and start something cooking. Those men will be after their coffee as soon as the talk starts to run down."

"Rose, I've asked Jed to call me Ellie and most times he remembers but sometimes he still says Miss Ellie. I want you to call me Ellie. I've felt like I've known you since I got that note. You should have seen me. I got Jed to take me to a little party at the local school house and on the way home things sure did take off. Later, when we got home and after I got inside so Jed couldn't see me, I looked up at the ceiling and I said, *thank you, sister Rose*."

"Here's a pan and here's some bacon. You get started on that while I get the coffee started. We've got eggs again since the weather warmed and some new bread so I guess we can fix you up with something."

"Rose, this will be fine if we can get Jed away from your father and Del long enough to eat."

After they had eaten, Rose was kind of flustered about

where they would put Jed and Ellen to sleep but Jed insisted they would be fine in the barn.

"We've got blankets with us, Rose. We'll just put one under us and the rest over top and if that isn't enough, we'll cover up with straw. We'll root in like two pigs. Let's go, Ellie and see how you are at living it rough."

After the long, hard day, Ellie snuggled up next to Jed and slept soundly. She never woke till Jed started stirring around in preparation to getting up.

"You awake, Miss Ellie?"

"Just."

"Sure going to be cold when we crawl out of here so we'd best make a list of things we're gonna do as soon as we hit the cold air."

"The first thing I need is that outhouse I saw out back. That's after I find my heavy coat. Then I'll head for the kitchen and help Rose get everybody's breakfast."

"I guess I'll get dressed and help Del feed the stock. You ready."

"As much as I'll ever be."

"Then throw the covers at the count of three. One, two, three. Hit decks a runnin'."

When Jed left the barn, he found everything had been done. The stock was fed and the eggs had been gathered. Ben, Del and Jack were all in Ben's little cabin waiting for the call to breakfast.

"Good mornin', everyone. I guess I overslept."

"Not by much. I get up in the mornin' and start the fire and then we men feed the stock while the house warms up. Then Rose gets up with the children and makes our breakfast."

"We have some time to talk then. Charlie told me in town that John had a hard winter."

Ben took a moment before he answered.

"Jed, I can't tell you how hard! He wasn't prepared and he didn't have enough hay. I'll have to say he tried. He got through the first blizzard without too much loss but we got a second one just a couple of weeks later. The only cattle he had left were a few that were still up here on Del's place. They found the piles of corn stocks and straw that Del had piled behind the barn and we didn't have the heart to drive them away from it even though we might have run short ourselves."

"I rode over to the *Rocking O* maybe two weeks ago. There was cattle layin' everywhere and the sky black with buzzards. John was drunk out of his skull. I sobered him up enough to talk to him. I asked him what he planned. He said California Sunshine, that's what he wanted. He said I could have the ranch back if I wanted it. I didn't want it, don't have the money to restock anyhow. I did give him five hundred dollars for the three *Rocking O* branding irons and the right to use the brand. I figured you might want to keep the brand goin' down there in Texas."

"It's a thought, Papa. We could use two brands, that's not illegal. Right now, we're using the brand Ellie's father registered so it will be up to her."

"Well, you take those irons with you when you go. There won't be any more *Rocking O* cattle around here. Del has already registered a *Rocking R* as his brand."

Just then Rose called for them to take breakfast so they all headed for the house.

"Hey, Jack, where's that big dog?"

"He's probably out gettin' his breakfast somewhere. He likes his independence."

"When he gets back, I think you should introduce me and Ellie then I'll tell you about the dog we have at our place. He saved my life twice within ten minutes though he's not as big as Rufe."

There wasn't much talk while they were having breakfast except for *pass me this* or *pass me that* but as soon as they'd finished eating, the men retired back to Ben's cabin.

"How do things look here, Del? Did you lose any stock at all?"

"No, we had everything in close and we rationed what hay we had. We had no idea that the cattle would eat those corn stalks. Apparently the stalks start to break down after they're piled high and they heat up and ferment, I guess. I won't depend on that but it will sure keep my mind at ease knowin' that cattle will eat it, if they're hungry enough. We've got what heifers we traded for last fall and they're startin' to calve and we have about thirty head of mixed stuff of John's that pulled through by eating corn stalks. John told Ben to keep them."

"Let's hear about what you've tied into down there in Texas, Jed. I don't suppose the winter hurt you none?"

"Not this year, though Ellie says some years you need hay. Thank God this year was good. We didn't get a chance to put up hay last summer. There's lots of timber on the place and I figure to get a tie contract with the railroad and put the boys to work at that in the winter."

"You said your dog saved your life. Let's hear the story on that."

"It was that Artie Smith I told you about last fall. He really got a spite on me and he ambushed me after he'd spent two months practisin' with a rifle ... shooting off his left shoulder, one handed. Just as Artie pulled the trigger, that dog nipped the heels of my horse and the horse jumped head. The bullet creased Stan's horse. He was on the far side of me. You should have seen that man ride.

"I got out of the way and this Artie was so full of spite he came out of his cover and started to where I was. Stan had bailed out of his saddle with his long gun and he shot Artie through the left elbow. Artie fell and busted that shoulder loose that I shot up last summer.

"Now he's down and his rifle is somewhere down below him. He's so full of hatred, somehow he makes that right arm work and he gets his side gun out and he hides it till Stan and I are not more than fifteen feet away then he tries for a shot but that dog's been watchin' him. When he moves that gun to fire, the dog jumps and grabs his hand and he misses. And do you know what, the dog bite killed him in the end. It was hardly more than a scratch. No one thought to tell the doctor about it, Artie had so much else wrong. Two days later, he got blood poisoning from the dog bite and he died from it."

A week went by so quickly that Ellen was surprised when Jed told her they needed to pack up and go back to town the next day.

"The roads have dried out now, Ellie and we'll go past the *Rocking O* on our way to Cheyenne. At least you will know where I grew up."

Early the next morning, they were on their way to Cheyenne.

"Rose told me Papa Ben gave you the *Rocking O* branding irons and a transfer paper from John that gives you the right to the registered brand."

"I thought you might agree to let me use both brands on our stock. That way the *Rocking O* brand wouldn't just die out."

"Jed, brand them all with the *Rocking O* irons. Father had no heritage to preserve with the brand we use and neither do I. From now on, it will be an Owens' wielding the branding iron so go ahead and register it as our brand."

"Miss Ellie, I don't know what to say except you know how to make me very happy. Let's get home to the new *Rocking O* Ranch in Texas."

TEXAS BOUND   Arnold McKay